THE LION OF GALLOWAY

A Historical Novel of Scotland

ARCHIBALD THE GRIM

J R TOMLIN

Albannach Publishing

Book cover by EbookLaunch.com

Proofreading by wordrefiner.com

❀ Created with Vellum

MAP OF MEDIEVAL SCOTLAND

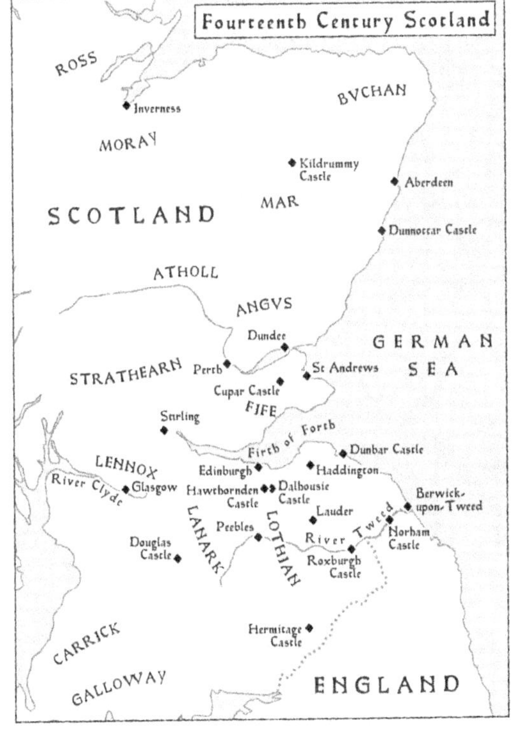

CHAPTER ONE

January 1359, Edinburgh Castle

As I strode toward the door, the noise of chatter filtered in from the bailey. A lamp hanging from a sconce threw flickering light across the hall. A deep voice called out from behind me. "Archie." I turned with a start. My cousin, William Douglas, Earl of Douglas, motioned for me to join him in a chamber.

The small, shadowy chamber with several kists stacked against one wall was certainly not his own. Had he hidden here merely to wait for me? Or had another meeting drawn him there? Curious, I bowed. "Aye, my lord?" I considered congratulating him on the King making him an earl but decided to wait and see what he was up to.

He patted my shoulder with a heavy hand, a forced smile curving his lips. "You should ken that there arenae hard feelings that you left my household to join the king. I understand why you did."

"I swore fealty to him when he knighted me. I was obliged to obey his summons." There was no reason to mention that I had prayed for the chance.

His hand still on my shoulder, he squeezed. "But I am

head of the house of Douglas. You have obligations to me and our ilk. Do you need to be reminded of that?"

Did he truly know me so little that he did not realize that my first loyalty was to the king? I opened my mouth to tell him he mistook me, then closed it. Sometimes it was wise to keep the truth behind my teeth. Moreover, I needed to learn exactly what he was asking of me. "Of course, I ken my duty to my family. How is it you think I am failing my obligations?"

"I didnae say you are failing. I merely remind you that you must be loyal to our ilk first. You are in a position to learn whatever goes on in the king's councils." His dark eyes narrowed. "He resents that my power and that of Angus and Stewart are much greater than his. He will act against us. But what will he do? I need you to apprise me of his plans. I must be prepared to defend myself, whatever he does."

My heart thudded, and I stroked my short, pointed beard. Whatever one might say about the Earl of Douglas, he was no fool. The king's power was seriously weakened after ten years as an English prisoner. I had never questioned that my cousin, along with Robert Stewart, Earl of Strathearn, and Thomas, Earl of Angus, would do whatever they could to keep it that way. This was the plot he wanted to draw me into. "I shall remember and do my duty, my lord. You may be certain of that." He could interpret that as siding with him if he cared to. I tilted my head toward the door to the bailey. "We shouldnae be late."

"Go," he said. "I must join my lady wife."

I bowed, returned to the corridor, and exited the outer door. A colorful throng was gathered in the upper bailey when I exited the outer door. The sun, only slightly above the walls of Edinburgh Castle, shined through scudding clouds and gave a sparkle to gems on hats, necks, and fingers. Puissant nobles were being ushered in first, according to rank, to go to the high table. A steady murmur of good-natured chatter filled the air. Standing there, I smoothed the front of my new black velvet doublet.

There had been little feasting on King David de Bruce's return three months ago from his captivity in England. He had felt it would be poorly received with the immense cost of his ransom, but a feast had been called for with the council ending in general agreement on who would keep lands they had acquired in the king's absence and which laws to amend.

First in was Robert Stewart, Earl of Strathearn, High Steward of Scotland, and heir to the throne, the king's nephew, less impressive than he might have been with his medium height, several years older than his own uncle. He had been the last to arrive for the council that had begun a week before. Only the news that the King was confirming the Stewart's possession of the earldom of Strathearn that was not rightfully his. King David had used it to try to convince the Earls of Douglas and Angus and the Stewart that they had nothing to fear from his return.

I nudged Will Ramsay with my shoulder when my cousin swaggered past, his wife on his arm, and was bowed inside. "Once you are married to the Countess of Fife, you will outrank him." I winked. "And you will be much too fine to speak to the likes of me."

"Not any time soon. We only just sent an appeal to the pope to give us dispensation for our kinship."

"I didnae realize you were kin."

He blew out a scornful *pfffffft*. "Only to the third degree. It should be nae problem to have him sign. Anyroad, you will outdo me given time. You underestimate yourself. Besides, I will only be Earl of Fife, jure uxoris, which hardly counts." Will rubbed his hands together, and his words were ghosted with smoke. "I wish the heralds would hurry with it. My toes are near frozen."

"Och, it counts, and I dinnae look so high. But I havenae complaints. The King has promised me more than I ever thought to receive." I scratched my cheek. "Have you met the lady of Fife yet?"

"Nae." Will shook his head. "But John Preston was the guest of her late husband. He says she is fair enough and seemed good-natured." Then he shrugged.

The King wantcd the match, so having met the lady was of no matter at all, as we both knew, so I changed the subject. "Anyroad, I heard that my cousin's new wife is already with child. That has him in fine spirits along with that earldom the King gave him."

"A new heir would sweeten his temper." He raised his eyebrow at me. We both knew Douglas hated that I was his heir until he had a son. "Being made an earl isnae much of a gift, though, if you ask me. Just a title and nae new lands."

"Aye, but it distracted him enough that he hardly even noticed that some of us are now the king's knights and nae longer in his following." I wrinkled my brow. Douglas had noticed more than I thought at first, but this was no place to mention his scheming. "And he is made Warden of the Western March as well, which carries considerable weight."

"Aye, he will be glad if that gives him an excuse to fight the English."

"The English want the rest of the money from the king's ransom to pay for their war in France, so they will abide by the truce." I glanced around. No one seemed to be listening, but there was no way to be sure. "But I have reason to believe that he and some others may be...plotting."

"Others?" Will lowered his voice. "Surely the Stewart is too big a coward for plots."

I glanced around again. "Later," I muttered.

A herald called Will's name and urgently motioned him in.

I wondered if King David was growing impatient because the rest of us were called to file in a moment later.

A page poured water over my hands and dried them. I paused when a familiar face stepped up. "James?" The last time I had seen James Douglas of Lothian, the Knight of Liddesdale's nephew, had been at Hermitage before his father's death.

James Douglas, barely twenty, with a thatch of auburn hair and a turned-up nose, gave a cheery grin. "Archie! You are a braw sight."

Plucking the herald's sleeve, I said, "James will sit with me."

The man scowled. "We would have to juggle the seating."

But moving one man would not upset their plans that much, so I said, "Then juggle it." I threw an arm around James's shoulder. "How have you been? I want to hear all."

The herald grudgingly led us to a place next to Will near the top of one of the long side tables. "Not at the high table, then?" I asked him.

"Nae, until I am married to the countess, I suppose. But I would sooner eat with friends than Robert Stewart's high-nosed wife."

I introduced my young cousin to him as puissant lords and their ladies took their places at the high table except by the king's and the queen's chairs in the middle. Of course, Robert Stewart had the place of honor next to the king.

Some light shined through the tall windows into the great hall, adding to the light from hundreds of candles in sconces on columns. Their beeswax scent mixed with the smell of perfume and burning oak logs. The gray stone walls were hung with banners: the red and gold lion rampant banner of the King of Scots, Scotland's blue and white Saltire banner, and the red and gold banner of the House of Bruce. Between were displayed crossed swords and war axes. Minstrels in the gallery played a clàrsach harp, viol, and lute that blended with the crackle of the fire in the enormous fireplace.

The chief herald shouted to announce the entrance of King David and Queen Joan. Trumpeters blew a flourish. The King entered with the queen on his arm. He wore a crimson silk surcoat with the royal lion rampant embroidered on the breast in gold, his brown beard neatly trimmed to a point. We all bowed, and he gave me a warm smile as he went by. Four years older than the king, the queen was stiff-faced with glittering blue eyes that angrily scanned the great hall for something, though I could not tell for what—or whom. He helped her up the steps to the dais, led her to her seat, and then nodded to William de Landallis, Bishop of Saint Andrews, who stood beside his chair.

A finely robed, plump man with angel-fine white hair around his tonsure, the bishop's eyes were assessing as he waited for silence to begin the blessing. After a brief prayer, we could finally take our seats. Toasts were made, and dishes were carried in so the feasting could begin. All was comfort and laughter—King David taking an enthusiastic part. The brightly clad company was in high good humor, with wine being poured freely. The best dishes, of course, were carried to the high table, but my goblet was filled with a fragrant, fruity claret, and a servant placed a tureen of peppered venison pottage, a platter with a fat roast capon, and almond cakes for us to share.

A troupe of tumblers ran in, the five men doing cartwheels as they came. They did flips, one over the other, and did handstands. Then they made a human pyramid, one at the top juggling balls before he leapt down, and they ran out, scooping up the coins thrown to them.

James said, "I heard your escape at Poitiers was a grand jest on the English."

I shook myself out of my reverie. "Aye, though the credit

goes to Will here for his wild tale. The English believed his story, though I wasnae sure he really had to tell them I was too ugly to be a noble."

"It worked, so dinnae complain." Will winked at James.

"But leaving the rest of you in their hands felt wrong."

"It wasnae so terrible. I had the chance for a few talks with King David. well worth a year in the tower." He shrugged. "We werenae ill-treated."

"That is good to hear." I turned to James. "Now, tell me what has happened to you since I last saw you."

He eagerly recounted his training as a squire, a small tourney he recently won against another squire, and that he hoped to convince King David to knight him. My attention wandered as he spoke.

Before the next course, a subtlety made of spun sugar shaped like the king's planned tower was carried in and paraded around the tables to enthusiastic cheers. Then fresh dishes were placed before us, and a peacock dressed in its feathers was served at the high table. I took only a few bites from each platter since even the lower tables were piled with food.

Minstrels entered, led by a man nearly as tall as I. He wore a green surcoat. Behind him came another young man and two women. One girl was as young and thin as a lad with only a small bosom. The other walked like a queen, young, tall, and shapely, dressed in emerald green velvet, perhaps eighteen. When she looked my way, her eyes were golden as molten honey, penetrating and watchful, but the corners crinkled. I could not look away. James watched her wide-eyed, and I could not blame him. She was the most beautiful woman I had ever seen.

Golden Eyes began to sing of unrequited love, her voice rich and perfect with the sparkling tones of the lute. She smiled at me, and suddenly I was out of breath, as though I had been punched in the stomach. I huffed. I would not make a fool of myself in front of the entire court, but oh, it was tempting.

When the King applauded, and I joined in, my cheek stretched in a smile that someone so beautiful made such enchanting music. He called for another song, and they followed with Ma Fin Est Mon Commencement and Rose, Liz, Printemps, Verdure. He sent them a purse, and they retired. My eyes followed as far as I could see. How might I find the minstrels again, particularly the one with the beautiful golden eyes? I shook myself, returned my mind to my friends, and told James I would speak to the King about him.

Our third course was served: shrimp tartlets, stored apples baked with honey, and cheeses. The hall grew noisy since the entertainment was over, and the wine flowed freely. Farther down our table, two men argued loudly, and a knight slumped face down at the opposite table.

At last, the King rose and commanded the floor cleared for dancing.

The side tables were pushed back and laid with bowls of almonds and steaming pitchers of hippocras, so I stood out of the way munching a few nuts and sipping the spiced wine. The minstrel began an estampie, singing about a squire's love for a beautiful lady. Still looking sullen, Queen Joan was led by the King onto the floor, and half a dozen other couples lined up below them for the first dance. They advanced to each other and linked arms. They whirled and glided to the bottom of the line to gay laughter. When the dance ended, they retired, and a more sedate rondel began. I looked around for someone to talk to since the ladies were partnered with their husbands.

Squirming with eagerness, a little page tugged my sleeve. "Sir, please, His Grace requires you."

I looked over the heads of the dancers. David was at the

end of the hall on the dais once more and speaking to a lovely lass, or rather from her headdress, a young woman. The Douglas listening, arms crossed and scowling. There was no sign of the queen, which was odd. I tossed the last couple of almonds into my mouth and motioned for the lad to lead the way.

The King beamed as I bowed. "Ha! Archie, my old friend." He looked to the side and nodded to the herald, who clapped his hands. My heart gave a jump. He had promised me a position, but I had not expected it so soon or announced before the entire court.

There was a loud flourish from the trumpeters. The conversation ceased as though cut off with a knife.

David cast his gaze over the crowd to be sure he had everyone's attention. He put his hand on my shoulder. "My dear friend, the braw knight, Sir Archibald Douglas, I now name as Guardian of Edinburgh Castle and Sheriff of Lothian!" There was a buzz of comments around the hall, and Will raised his fist to me in triumph.

A muscle in Douglas's jaw jerked.

"Your Grace!" I knelt and bowed my head, which allowed me to hide the look of astonishment that must have been on my face. "You honor me with your trust, sire." I rose with a smile so big it made my cheeks ache.

"Have you mentioned to the Stewart that you are replacing his man?" Douglas asked.

"No. Why should I?"

"Replacing his appointment could be seen as a hostile act."

A corner of David's mouth curved up. "Och, but the positions of guardian of the castle and sheriff of Edinburgh are mine to appoint. My nephew would certainly nae dispute that."

"Aye, of course, Your Grace." His tone of voice was

friendly, but when he turned to me, the look in his eye was more of a dare. "Congratulations, Archie. I am sure you will ken what needs to be done." Then he abruptly bowed to the king, saying he should return to his lady wife.

David held out his hand to the lady beside him, ignoring the Douglas's departure. "My dearest Katherine Mortimer has only just arrived from Inverbervie, Archie. When she accompanied the queen, she was all that made my imprisonment there tolerable."

Katherine Mortimer was certainly bonnie enough. More than bonnie, a beauty. It was common gossip that the King had a mistress while he was imprisoned in England, but I had not heard that she had arrived in Edinburgh. Since most nobles had at least one bastard, including the Stewart, who had a parcel of them, none could criticize having a mistress. But it was no wonder the queen had been purse-mouthed and retired so early. The arrival of his mistress would set the cat amongst the pigeons. She was the daughter of Sir Roger Mortimer of Inverbervie and had traveled to England as Queen Joan's lady-in-waiting. Her influence in the bedchamber would be a worry, especially if she had a child.

"Sir Archibald, His Grace has spoken of you often with much kindness." She had a soft, attractive voice. She seemed only about twenty, with delicately molded features held erect on a long, graceful neck. Beneath high eyebrows flashed laughing eyes. She clapped her hands with delight. "Och, another dance is beginning."

David held out his hand. "And you havenae yet danced, sweet lady, so we must mend that."

"But what about the brave Sir Archibald?" A mischievous smile curved her lips, and she motioned to a young woman nearby. "I ken. He must partner, dearest Joanna de Moravia, Lady of Bothwell."

I flinched with no idea whether the young woman would

even want to dance with me, but there was no choice but to bow and offer her my hand. She tilted her head and gave a graceful curtsy as she laid her fingers on mine. "You honor me, sir."

I led her down the steps of the dais, following the King and Katherine, glancing at the lady beside me from the corner of my eye. Of course, the daughter of Maurice of Moravia, the king's close friend who had died at Neville's Cross. She had married one of the de Murrays, a hostage in England to guarantee payment of the king's ransom. She was not a beauty as Katherine Mortimer might be said to be, but seemed pleasant enough, though no doubt missing her husband.

Joanna moved easily and smoothly to the quick rhythm of the estampie, and I was grateful that I remembered the steps. "You are joining the king's household, Lady Joanna?" I asked.

"Aye, the queen needs ladies to serve her, and I will be one of them. Since Katherine is otherwise occupied." She wrinkled her brow, looking doubtful. "I hope that works out well."

I could not think of any reply to that. She was in the middle of what could be a dangerous tangle of courtly intrigue. That was the sort of battle I preferred to stay well out of. But as we went through the steps of the dance, I felt Douglas's eyes stabbing my back.

CHAPTER TWO

The seneschal, an upright, dignified man with a shock of gray hair, produced a large ring of keys from his belt and opened the door to the outer chamber of the guardian's apartment.

The wind rattled the shutters, and the two tapestries on the wall did little to stop the chill that permeated the stone walls. There was a faint smell of damp stone, but a fire crackled in the small fireplace, and the rushes on the floor were fresh. At the far end of the room was another door, leading no doubt to the bedchamber.

Making chambers livable had never been one of my concerns. I wondered how one went about such a thing.

He walked to a table strewn with parchments, a box of quills, an ink bottle, an unlit candle, and sealing wax. He took a large key from his scrip and laid it on the table. "This will open the lock of the outer and inner chamber, Sir Archibald." He twisted his bony hands together, looking past me over my shoulder. "I have the working of the servants and laborers well in hand, so there isnae need for you to fash yourself with it."

The servants and domestic arrangements were his business, but from his nerves, perhaps the previous governor had interfered. Or was it that he feared I might find if I interfered? "I havenae doubt you do." I strolled over to pick up the key. "Those minstrels at the feast yestereve. You hired them?"

"Was there a problem with them?" his voice went up. "They are from Poitier, I am told, and have performed for the French nobles. So they say, anyroad. They were highly recommended, but if they offended—"

I cut off his blathering. "Not at all. Sir William Ramsay told me he is seeking mummers for his wedding celebration. Not many are to be found in Scotland these days, so I thought..." Now I was blathering, so I stopped. Being in a position of command, having no one to answer to but the King would take time to adjust to. I had no need to explain why I asked. "They did well, so I want their names and location."

"Aye, Sir Archibald." With a look of relief, he went on." They stay at a house down a vennel next to the White Hart Inn. I think it is shared with some minstrels."

That was good to know, but it would be undignified for the new sheriff of Edinburgh to call on mummers. Despite my lie about Will's wedding, I had no excuse to hire them. But I would have to figure something out if I wanted to see her again. I definitely did.

"Good." Bouncing the key in my hand, I said, "That will be all for now. We will discuss the castle finances when I have had time to settle in."

That had him looking anxious again. He made obeisance and scurried for the door with assurances that there was no need to bother me with such things. No doubt he skimmed some of the castle funds and was hoping I would forget the matter. All seneschals did, I had been told.

The lock to the bedchamber turned easily. Thick bed

hangings surrounded the bed, so it should be warm enough even in winter. Against the wall was a large kist painted with two knights jousting amongst some trees. Rubbing my chin, I started a list of what I would need. Another kist would be first on the list. That one would barely hold my armor. But there were ample pegs for hanging my weapons.

The door creaked slightly as it opened, and Gil, a chunky, fairish man, stuck in his head. "Good." He pushed the door the rest of the way open with his shoulder, his arms filled with a leather bag containing armor, and puffed slightly as he entered. "I was hoping the guard pointed me in the right direction."

"There is a kist we can use and pegs. They will suffice for now."

"Aye, it is much to get accustomed to." He lugged the bag to the kist, raised the lid, and dumped it inside.

"Bring up both of our clothes." I tugged my earlobe. "Look in the storage for a paillasse. A brazier. A folding stool. Tell the seneschal I said so if need be."

Gill rubbed his hands, beaming. "I will see to it. Dinnae fash!" He hustled out.

Although I had spent the last months as one of the king's household knights, there had been neither reason nor opportunity to become acquainted with the functionaries whose duties had nothing to do with me. I strode to the door and ordered the man-at-arms outside to find the constable, Simon Reed, and order him to attend to me. As an afterthought, I also commanded him to bring his chief assistant. I had only seen the constable briefly when I was introduced as the new sheriff. A spare, thin-faced man with the bearing of one accustomed to command, he looked to be in his middle age, his hair graying and receding at the forehead.

After shoving the high-backed chair near the fireplace, I put two stools where I could see the men when they were seated. I shivered and sat to stretch my feet out onto the hearthstone and the welcome heat. I scowled at the tapestries again and wondered how one went about finding more to lessen the chill.

When there was a knock on the door, I called for them to enter. The guard opened the door, and Reed followed with his assistant. I raised an eyebrow at the assistant, for I rarely saw someone as tall as myself. His shock of ginger hair ran down as side whiskers to join his roughly trimmed beard. In his battered chainmail, I suspected no lawbreaker in Edinburgh would give him any trouble.

Reed bowed and said, "At your service, my lord."

I breathed a snort. "Dinnae bother with 'my lording' me. I am nae lord and dinnae use titles that arenae mine. It is Sir Archibald."

The constable's eyes widened in surprise. "As it pleases you, Sir Archibald. This is my serjeant, Rauf of Herth."

Rauf tugged his forelock, though the look in his eye was less than subservient.

"The service I need right now is an explanation of how the castle and burgh are running and what I need to know about any problems we will face." I waved a hand to the stools. "So, sit and first tell me what you think I need to hear." I was sure they would not be forthcoming with any genuine problems, but I had to make a start somewhere. "Start with the taxes." I restrained a sigh as Reed went over customs duties on wool and leather, stall tax, gate tax, and fees for repairing the city walls, but he assured me that on Candlemas in a few weeks, most would pay. From how he said it, plainly, that was not all would. "Any who are slow to pay, I send Rauf and a few of his men to remind them."

I raised my eyebrow at the mild wording of a reminder.

Rauf smirked. "Few need more than me and two of my men to appear at their door."

"And I trust Rauf to deal with any who dare to break the king's peace," Reed concluded.

The serjeant shrugged his heavy shoulders. "We havenae more nor less of lawbreakers than any burgh. Mostly cutpurses on market day, or some beggar may steal a chicken for his pot. A stooshie in a tavern after too much strong ale, we use our truncheons to break up. A drunk may be knocked out for his script. Sometimes, a man may take a rod to his wife so hard that she dies, and that will be for you to see hanged. Sure, and there is a knifing now and then, but the killer confesses fast enough. Whores, my men make sure they stay off the street, and if they are caught, then they be whipped at the merket square. What they do out of sight though isnae porridge of mine, as I sees it."

I raised a skeptical eyebrow. "No thefts worse than a cutpurse or chicken thief in the whole of Edinburgh?"

"Aye, at times a burgher will have something stolen out of his shop, but most keep a guard or two, so there is less than you would think. The guards mostly catch the thief and drag him in when there is. Outwith the city walls now, 'tis another thing. The Turnbulls are getting right bold in their reiving. They dinnae care if they rob from Sassenach or us. They have raided into Edinburgh's shrievdom a few times recently. I wouldnae mind seeing some of that lot hang. But some of them be too powerful to touch since they fought for the king."

"I am glad to hear there arenae problems for me to handle. Not that I am any too sure I am hearing all the truth, but if you keep the peace and bring me the taxes, I willnae interfere too much." I slapped my knee and stood. "I think I will look about the burgh. Mayhap stop at the White Hart for a cup of ale to let people see the new sheriff."

Both men stood.

"You arenae going alone, Sir Archibald?" Reed looked appalled.

"Nae, I will have a few men with me, and you are welcome to join us. There might be trouble spots for you to point out." I needed to talk to Colbyn about what I would want of him, and Gil deserved a cup of ale for all his work. It would be a chance to talk to James about joining the following that I must build. I was sure the King would knight him out of respect for the Ramsays, though he would want to wait for an appropriate occasion, no doubt. And if some mummers living nearby happened to come in for a drink, that would also suit me well.

CHAPTER THREE

February 1359

In the next weeks, two visits to the White Hart had brought no sign of the golden-eyed lassie. The weather was mild, so the King rode out with Katherine Mortimer by his side, flying their hawks, accompanied by a score of his household knights. Somehow, Queen Joan was never invited. There was gossip that she had written to her brother in England for permission to visit her mother at Hertford Castle. I suspected she would be in no hurry to return if she did.

Two days after Candlemas, early February, it was a crisp, clear morning, and I would have preferred to ride out hawking this morning when King David, his mistress, and their companions left rather than bending the counting cloth and stacks of coin in the squares to keep track with Walter Reed. A narrow-faced cleric's quill scratched at a parchment as he recorded the tally. Penny by penny, we went over a record of the taxes that had been collected, Candlemas being a quarter day when taxes must be paid. My head was throbbing. A large, iron-bound kist with two locks held the hundreds of silver pennies that would go to the king's treasury, except for a small portion that was my due.

There was a rap on the door, and I called out permission to enter.

Rauf of Herth pushed the door open. "The prior from Newbattle Abbey be here with news, sir."

Welcoming the interruption, I turned with a smile that failed when I saw the pale-faced cleric.

Small and frail looking, he wrung his hands in distress as he delivered his tidings. "It was at the sixth hour, my lord sheriff, and the lay brothers in the fields were still at their prayers, about to move the cattle to a different field. Men attacked them! Killed two of the brothers."

"What?" A hot flush of anger went through me. "Who were they? English?"

"We dinnae ken, Sir Archibald, but the lay brother said they were Scots. The other was too injured to speak. More than a score, he said. That was the best he could tell us."

"None of them were recognized?" Attacking a monastery was bad enough, but this was a stab at both the King and me.

The prior tucked shaking hands into the wide sleeves of his habit. "The lay brothers ran as fast as they could to hide in the nearby woods. It is by the grace of God that they escaped." He took a deep breath, as though working up his courage. "The abbot begs that you take action. These murderous reivers must be stopped and examples made of them, else who kens what will be next."

I scowled, my mind racing. "Aye, the abbey is far from the border for the English reivers to attack. But that Scots would attack a monastery..." I slammed my fist on the table. The parchments bounced, and Reed grabbed the inkwell to keep it from spilling. "Wherever they came from, by Saint Bride, I give you my oath that they will be punished."

"Thank you, my lord."

There was no point in pointing out that I was not a lord. It did not matter. I had a duty. Newbattle Abbey had been founded by the king's namesake and grandsire to the fifth generation, King David, the first of that name. David would take an attack on the abbey and killing lay brothers as a direct insult to the crown and a sign of lawlessness. And the boldness of attacking an abbey so near Edinburgh demanded immediate action.

"I shall lead some of my men-at-arms to track them down myself. The monasteries will be protected!" I softened my rough tone, realizing the prior was sagging with exhaustion. "Rauf, take the prior to the hall and see he has food and drink. And send word to Colbyn to attend me at once."

Rauf bobbed his head.

"We will escort you back to the abbey," I said to the prior. "There, we will pick up the thieves' tracks, and I mean to see they are punished."

A look of relief crossed the prior's face. He made obeisance. I shook my head. It would take a long time to become accustomed to receiving such courtesies.

'What about the taxes?" the constable asked.

"They must wait until I return. I cannae see that tracking them down will take more than a few days. Be sure that Rauf and his men collect any that hasnae been paid. It cannae go to the king's treasury until that is done, anyroad."

"Can you overtake them, though? They have a large head start."

"Aye, if we move at a good pace, which I intend to. They can move at most ten or twelve miles a day herding cattle. We can ride more than triple that, but we cannae delay."

My grizzled old friend, Colbyn, trotted in with Gil on his heels. "There was an attack?"

"Gil, lay out my heavy clothes and cloak. Pack my armor and yours as well." Then I turned to Colbyn. "We ride out within the hour. Summon a score of men-at-arms and a couple of scouts and send word to James Douglas and John

Preston to be ready to ride with us. A spare horse for every man for his armor and food."

"Aye, Sir Archibald." Colbyn was never so formal if we were alone or only with Gil, but he would never risk showing disrespect before others. He turned and stomped out the door, and Gil scurried into the bedchamber. I did not need to give either more specific commands.

Gil was quick after squiring for me for several years, so he made quick work of packing our armor, beaming for the chance to ride out. He would load it onto a sumpter so we could wear thick woolen clothes and cloaks through the winter chill. We would don armor if needed for a fight.

I loped down the stairs and into the bailey yard. It contained the stone chapel built by Saint Margaret and wood sheds and buildings, some barracks, other stables, store-rooms, and a kitchen.

The prior scrambled clumsily into the saddle of his sleek palfrey, and I hoped he was a good enough horseman not to slow us down. My men were smiling and joking, looking eager to miss sentry duty for what should be a pleasant ride. Horses jibbed and shook their jingling tack as the men joked about what they would do to the thieves when we caught up to them. Even if we were outnumbered, judging by the priors' report, well-armed men-at-arms would have little trouble against outlaws with rusty swords, knives, and clubs, so they looked forward to what should be an easy fight.

The groom brought my mount, and I swung into the saddle. With Preston riding next to me, we led my men out the main gate and down the royal way through the busy streets of Edinburgh. Gil shouted for them to make way, and they scurried to let us pass. The royal banner and my own streamed from the force of our passing. I set my heels to my horse's flanks and rode at a canter. It was not an ideal time for beginning the hunt with the sun nearing its height in the clear sky, but if we were to have any hope of catching up with the thieves, we could not delay. The roads were dry since we had had little rain, and a crisp white cloud cast a shadow over the Lammermuir Hills to the south. Alternating a canter with a walk, we were making good time. I sent outriders to our flanks and scouts, taking no chances of riding into an ambush. At least a herd of cattle would be no trouble to track even over the dry ground, for the last few weeks had seen no rain.

The prior grunted and occasionally groaned as we rode, but when Preston asked how he fared, he replied he was offering the discomforts of a day in the saddle as a sacrifice for the souls of the slain brothers. One of the men began singing a bawdy tavern song, but Corbyn ordered them to shut it. They grumbled but obeyed. A kestrel lazily circled overhead and swooped down, catching a small bird on the wing.

Our pace remained brisk as we descended into the valley along the South River Esk, and the stone walls and buildings of the abbey spread before us.

Gil's stomach grumbled loudly. "I dinnae suppose we can take time to eat our bread and cheese before we ride on," he said morosely.

I smiled. My stomach was grumbling as well. "Our mounts must be watered and have a few minutes' rest if we are to keep up this pace. The abbot may even spare us some of their braw ale."

Gil's expression cheered as I put my heels to my horse's flanks and sped toward the thick wooden gate of the abbey. The porter pulled them open with a shout of thanksgiving.

When we rode into the inner court, the tall and dignified Abbot William stepped around the two monks he had been conferring with, raising his hands in either thanksgiving or blessing, which I could not tell.

"God's blessings on you, Sir Archibald. I beg you tell me that His Grace has sent you to succor us in our distress."

I urged my mount a few steps forward, dismounted, and made my obeisance. "Father Abbot, I will track them down myself. The King would expect no less, but we need our horses watered and my men refreshed before we ride on. Also, one of the brothers must show us where the attack took place."

The abbot ordered lay brothers to tend to the horses and the cellarer to provide the men with pitchers of ale, freshly baked bread, and cheese. Once their brief repast was washed down, I ordered a remount. A burly lay brother shuffled his feet, looking not at all happy to be sent to the scene of such violence but made no demure when a man-at-arms hauled him up behind his saddle to ride pillion. We rode away with the abbot's blessings following us.

The brother had us halt in a field still rutted from last year's plowing, only a short ride away from the abbey proper. He climbed from the horse's rump and pointed to where the sod was broken and torn.

"We move them to the fields for the stubble from last year's crop as feed and to feed the soil. We were about to move them to another field..." He swallowed. "They didnae need to kill them. We arenae knights! We wouldnae have fought them!"

"I will see they pay for their crimes," I said.

He shook his head. "Only the Lord God can exact a high enough price. Poor Liam hurt no one, one of the Lord's gentle lambs..." Shaking his head again, he turned and walked back toward the abbey, his robes flapping about his shanks.

Colbyn, one of the best serjeants a man could have, ordered our outriders to our flanks and sent scouts cantering ahead. Even with the sod frozen, a hundred cattle would be easy to track, and the reivers would know it. I had no intention of riding into a trap. The brief night was warm enough that all that we needed was a small cook fire for cooking oat bannocks on iron plates we carried.

Our quarry had moved slowly with the herd of cattle, so we were not far behind by the time the sun was straight overhead, but we were in disputed lands controlled by the English. I doubled our outriders. Colbyn returned from riding with the scouts, and I called a halt at the top of a hill with thick woods at the end of a slope. "They split. Cattle turned east. Most of the riders turned south, following the road into the hills." Ahead, the trees of the forest closed around the way.

I chewed my lower lip. We could recover the cattle, but the leader would most likely be with that group, and they might be headed toward more plunder. Stopping them and bringing them to the king's justice was more important than cattle. And I wanted men to hang to show that I could be counted on for justice, something I could not ignore.

"You ride ahead with the scouts," I told him. "I want to take them unawares, so bring me news."

He looked overhead, squinting in the noonday sun. The days were still short, so there were only four hours until dark. "Still some time while it is light." He gave me a wry smile. "I dinnae ken what you decides, but if you move closer to the woods so's to be close to attack, I'm sure I can find you, Sir Archibald."

Nodding, I stifled a grin at his hint. "I am sure you can, Colbyn."

I was more worried that I recognized these hills. We were where we ambushed the English with the aid of the French years ago and dangerously near the English-held Norham Castle. The English claimed this part of the border, though we disputed that claim. We needed to finish this business and turn back as soon as might be.

At the bottom of the hill, we set up a horse line where there was dried grass they could feed on. I decided against a fire. In the summer heat, we would be comfortable enough. The men shared out some cheese and stale bannocks as we waited. The light had faded as dark as it would get on the brief summer night when Colbyn and the two scouts returned. "They set up camp in a clearing a wee mite off the road. From the tracks, I thinks a score of them, but they had sentries set so we couldnae sneak close."

"Sentries? How many?"

Domhnall, a wiry scout with a weathered face, said, "I saw two, but that was only on the near side of the camp."

When Colbyn nodded in agreement, I rubbed my stubbly chin and pondered. "Whoever is leading them kens what he is doing. These dinnae seem like starving outlaws robbing with rusty swords and staves."

"Seems like you're right," Colbyn said.

"How far into the woods is their camp?"

"A half hour at a walk."

"So, five minutes at a gallop." I turned and surveyed our men, none of them who had followed me in the days when we had stalked the English through the woodlands. "We will have to ambush them on the road. Preston, I want you to circle through the woods with half our men to get ahead of them far enough to be out of sight when they return to the road. Colbyn can show you how far. I will lead an attack on their rear as soon as they are back on the road. I will give a shout that you can hear. If they make a stand, you join the attack. More likely, they will run themselves onto your swords." Even if they had better weapons and more skill than most outlaws, they would be no match for my well-armed and armored men and probably would flee. "Either way, we catch them between us and crush them. But remember, I want at least a few alive to hang."

"Might it not be better to attack them tonight when they are camped?" Sir John Preston said.

Colbyn turned to him with a scornful twist of his lip. "With all our men clanking in mail and ne'er a one of them experienced in sneaking. Except me and Sir Archibald, I means. They would give us away sure as sunrise on the morrow."

Preston nodded in surprisingly easy acceptance of this reply.

"I need one of the scouts hidden near the road to gallop back with word as soon as they are on the move."

Colbyn tilted his head toward Domhnall. "He is the best for the job."

"Aye, sir, I can do that easy enough. Some hawthorns can screen me and my mount. I can gallop back as soon as they is out of sight."

CHAPTER FOUR

When the first sliver of pewter light edged the eastern horizon, I ordered the men into their armor and to be ready to mount. The sky had barely lightened when Domhall galloped out of the trees, clods of dirt flying from under his horse's hooves. "They is moving!" He took a gulp of air. "I counted thirty. Not in any hurry."

"Mount up!" I shouted and leapt into the saddle. We were outnumbered. Still, surprise and our armor and weapons would give us the advantage. We formed up three abreast, as wide as the road.

With legs and hands, I urged my horse to a fast canter and then to a gallop, the rumble of running horses following close behind. The minutes passed slowly. We moved down a slight incline hedged by hawthorns between hoary oaks. Suddenly, the thieves, on small horses, were before us.

They outnumbered us by over two to one, and their leader made a fast decision. They turned to fight, a smart move on his part. I drew my sword, missing a lance that was better for fighting on horseback. As they charged, I bellowed, "A

Douglas! A Douglas!" and lowered my sword to use like a lance. Behind me, Gil took up the shout.

One thief swung a bludgeon at me. I ducked under it, and the force of our horses rammed my sword into his armpit nearly up to the hilt. As I fought to free my blade, Gil kicked him in the chest, driving him off his horse. The body slid, jerking my claymore from my hands, and I cursed. A burly, red-haired thief in battered mail stood in his stirrups and whaled at a man-at-arms. He nudged his heavy roan sideways, making way for more men to push through to attack.

I loosed my foot from the stirrup and kicked the horse in the mouth. It reared, but the redhead stuck the saddle on the jittering mount and raised his sword to strike. I flung my arms up, crossed, and blocked the strike with my plate-covered arms. As it jarred me back, I grabbed his wrists and threw myself at him, unseating him from his horse. We plummeted to the ground in a flurry of thrashing limbs.

Dazed, I rolled free and scrambled to my knees, swaying. He was nearly as big as me and recovered faster. He slammed a mailed fist into the side of my head, ringing my helm like a bell. My ears were ringing, and there were spots in front of my eyes when he launched himself at me, knocking me flat on my back. Straddling my hips, he put his full weight on me and pressed down on my mail-clad throat, my dagger trapped under his knee. I did not need to see his other hand to know he was going for his dagger. A thrust through the eye slots of my helm would finish me.

Just before the blade reached my face, I jerked my head and turned it. The blade scraped as I worked the round-bladed rondel free. I sunk it to the hilt into his mail-clothed side, the narrow blade sliding into the openings in the links. He coughed, blood splattering from his mouth. He raised his arm for another strike, but a mail-booted foot kicked him off me. Lying on the ground, he looked up in bewilderment.

James reached down and hoisted me to my feet. "Sorry. It took a minute to cut my way through." He grinned at me and pointed. Preston and his men had hit the thieves from the rear. The thieves were trapped, and the few left alive desperately tried to free themselves.

Pulse pounding, I scanned the field. There was still work to do. I shook off Gil, who was trying to help me onto my mount. "I am nae hurt."

Putting my foot on my first opponent's chest, I jerked my claymore free and climbed into the saddle. "Try to take one alive!" I yelled. Colbyn reversed his blade and knocked one thief to the ground with a blow of his hilt. At least the King would have one to hang. I drew my sword again. One of my men took an axe blow in the back. The weapon hung, and as he tried to jerk it free, I hacked a side swing, taking the reiver from his neck and blood gushed. The fighting was incredibly hard for such a small fight compared to the Battle of Poitiers. They threw everything they could into fighting free, asking no quarter. They knew if they surrendered, only execution awaited. Men slashed and stabbed and died. One fought his way through and galloped into the shadows of the forest. One more followed. My men shouted and prepared to give chase, but I called them back. Two could do nothing, and the knowledge we were near Norham Castle itched like a rash.

Colbyn kicked over the body of the first man I had killed. "This is one of the Nixons."

"Have the men strip them of anything worth taking, and we will divide the loot when we make camp. Then I want them strung up by their necks. That should ensure everyone receives the message." I spat on the ground. "I will see what I can get out of our prisoner once we camp."

The men made quick work of it, and soon the bodies dangled from the nearby trees. A raven flapped onto a branch and called out its harsh *grunk grunk*. Another settled beside it to watch as we rode away.

I ordered to make camp where the reivers had stopped the night before. Colbyn dragged our single prisoner along to be secured, leaving the bodies to the scavengers. The men were exhausted, and some had wounds to be tended. Only one had died. We would rest and turn back for Edinburgh at first light. Just because the fighting was done did not mean my responsibilities were over. I had to take my men and our prisoner home.

A headache pounded behind my eyes from the blow to my head, but I dragged the prisoner, Rany, he told Colbyn his name was, to his feet and demanded to know who had ordered the raid. He spat at me. He had little reason to answer since he would hang whatever he might tell. I drew back my arm and hit him backhanded across the face. He landed flat on his back. Then I kicked him in the side.

"Does it matter who gave the orders?" Preston asked.

"I want to know."

Preston shrugged.

"I can have my men beat you bloody, knock out your teeth, and break your ribs before you hang. Or you can have a dry bed, a good meal in your belly, and even a priest to hear your confession." I drew back my foot and kicked him in the ribs. "It is up to you."

Gil cracked his knuckles. "I could give him a taste of it."

"I have naught to tell you." Rany spat a mouthful of blood on the ground. "I take orders. That be all."

"From the Nixons?"

"Aye, one of them. Wulle be a cousin three or four times removed from the lord."

"Who gave him orders? The lord?"

He just glared at me, so I shrugged. "Then you can go to

the gallows after my men beat you bloody and with an empty belly. I cannae say I care."

Still glaring, he said, "Doesnae matter if you ken, I suppose. A lord came to talk to Wulle. I heard him called Fergus MacDowell, so one of thon Galloway ilk. Wulle looked right pleased when he left and said we would be well paid for the raid." He spat again. "Nasty business killing monks. I tried to tell Wulle so."

"Why would a bull-pizzle MacDowell pay for a raid in Lothian?" I mused aloud.

Preston squinted and wrinkled his brow. "I suppose causing trouble in Galloway would do him no good. The lot of them yon, MacDowells, Agnews, McCollochs, and Adairs and God only kens who are with the English and supported Balliol. Cattle stealing there would be stealing from an ally."

I grunted, only response. He was right about Galloway, but we had problems enough without taking on one that thorny. We had been trying to bring Galloway under control since the days of the King David, the first of that name. If it happened, it would not be today.

CHAPTER FIVE

I turned in the saddle to look back south over the peaceful scene, the bloody battlefield now out of sight in the woods. This was the soft part of Scotland, soft hills studded with rocky outcroppings. Soon it would be draped in purple heather, dotted bushes covered in white and yellow blossoms hiding their prickles under their beauty, just as the land did. In all of Scotland, I found nowhere so lovely, and it was no wonder that the English coveted and claimed it was theirs. But it was the men I considered. Three men were bandaged from injuries, and one tied across his mount to be given rites at Edinburgh. I had a handsome bruise on my head to show for it. The prisoner, hands tied and feet lashed beneath his horse's belly, glowered as we rode toward his hanging. I had promised him a priest for confession before I hanged him. Our banners flopped listlessly in the faint breeze.

"A scout returning!" Preston pointed ahead.

Domhnall was galloping back, his horse's mane flying. "A company approaching," he called. "Three miles ahead. Twoscore, mounted and armored."

Armor would reveal itself in bright sunlight. "Could you tell who?"

"I made out the banner. Red with lion charge and a white border."

Sir Thomas Grey, governor of Norham Castle, a man I knew well since I had once taken him prisoner. "Devil take him." I had hoped to leave land claimed by the English without encountering them. There was a truce, and it was a truce that the King was determined would not be broken.

The men muttered uneasily. The horses jittered at jerked reins, and I heard the swish of blades against their leather scabbards as they were loosened. I turned my horse and shouted, "We will abide by the truce! So dinnae draw a blade except on my command!"

There was a slight chance their scouts had not spotted us, so I signaled us forward at a steady walk. The bright gold coin of the sun hardly warmed the winter chill, so our woolen clothes and cloaks were welcome. I hoped Sir Thomas did not give me a reason to regret that we had removed our armor.

A little while later, we topped one of the hills that dotted the landscape to view more hills ahead, and the English rode straight toward us. The knight in the lead was handsomely equipped and mounted, helm held on his bent arm, and his twoscore men-at-arms gleaming in the sun. I did not envy them cooking beneath the sun. I pulled up and waited for them to approach.

"Well, well, well." Grey grinned, eyes gleaming, and grizzled hair tousled from the ride. "If it is not Black Archibald himself."

I tilted my head in acknowledgment and chuckled at the name. It was not the first time I heard it. "Sir Thomas, well met," I replied in French. It always amused me that my French was considerably better than that of the proud descendants of the Norman conquerors of the English. Despite the twitches of nerves racing through my limbs, I kept my expression mild.

With a laugh, he said, "I doubt your sincerity in that sentiment." He held out a hand. "I would have your sword, and you are my prisoner."

I sighed and handed it over. "Rather than take us prisoner, thank us. The reivers I killed would as soon steal from the English as from us." I thrust my thumb over my shoulder. "And I am looking forward to hanging that one for their attack on Newbattle Abbey."

His men collected the weapons from the rest of my men but did not unbind our prisoner. Gil grumbled at handing over the Douglas banner he carried.

"That explains the cattle tracks. But I fear your lord owes me some recompense for the years it took to raise my ransom."

"That was no choice of mine, Sir Thomas, and the Earl of Douglas is no longer my lord. I serve King David." I continued, as he raised his eyebrows in surprise. "We make no resistance so as not to break the truce, but I hope we can come to an agreement—" I leaned toward him slightly, focusing on his face. "Might I suggest we retire somewhere we can speak?"

James opened his mouth to speak, but I shook my head. I did not want to chance anyone giving away that I was now the Sheriff of Lothian, which would substantially increase any ransom.

He gave a courteous tilt of his head, always a courtly knight. "It is not a far ride to Norham. I will listen to what you propose there."

He signaled his procession to proceed, and we rode toward the ford across the Tweed. Despite the embarrassing and difficult situation, which I did not look forward to explaining to the king, I was glad to have a chance to talk to

Sir Thomas. Douglas had set a huge ransom for him that had taken years to be paid, and he had been the object of gossip talk since it was paid.

I nudged my mount to ride beside him and cleared my throat. "Someone at Edinburgh told me you are writing a chronicle, Sir Thomas." I had never heard of anyone other than a monk writing such a thing. "Is that true?"

"And you think writing an unmanly pursuit, I suppose."

I snorted a laugh. "No one who ever fought you in battle, as I have, would call you unmanly. But I am curious."

"Curious?"

"Why you came to do something so...surprising."

"Aye, surprising." He snorted. "But I had little to do those many months as a prisoner in Edinburgh Castle, even with the freedom of the burgh. I read some chronicles at Holy-rood Abbey and thought it was time for someone who was actually there to tell what happened."

"You have the right of it there." I pondered. "A few churchmen know what battle is like, but rarely the men who sit in an abbey penning the tales." I chuckled. "Better you than me, though. I am no fine hand with words."

"The monks who have read what I've written have not been impressed, but I decided to finish what I started. I dislike leaving things half done."

We splashed across the ford, ice rimmed in the winter chill. Sir Thomas nodded to the square lump of Norham, a castle meant for defense with no sign of grace or embellishment. But then, it must have been attacked hundreds of times by one side or the other in our eternal wars.

Ramparts and a palisade topped the gray curtain walls, and a gatehouse where a drawbridge could be dropped across the deep moat, its slow-moving water coated with nasty-looking blue-green algae. The drawbridge creaked and groaned as it was lowered, and we rode into the bustling bailey. Grooms hurried out of a line of stables to take our mounts. Another score of men-at-arms was training with pikes, and a couple of archers practiced at the butts. Next to a wood kitchen hut with smoke rising from a chimney, a grizzled kitchen servant with a smudged face twisted a chicken's neck.

Like many keeps, the door was not on the ground floor but reached by a wooden forestair that could be thrown down in case of attack. We thumped them behind Sir Thomas while his men made their way to the barracks. The great hall was as plain as the castle itself, a thick layer of rushes on the floor, fresh enough to show he kept his servants at work, and the wooden trestle tables were scrubbed clean. Even the maister's seat at the dais table was plain wood, and the seating all benches. He threw himself down with a gusty sigh and shouted for wine. As a server set plain pewter cups of wine before us, he said, "Wash the dust from your throat and then tell me this proposal."

Preston sat next to me, looking curious and sipping his drink. James plunked down next to him, watching with wide-eyed curiosity.

I drained the cup of the sour wine and leaned my elbows on the table. "I doubt me that you want to feed and house us while you wait for our ransom."

He shrugged. "It would be little trouble to hang him."

"True, but why bother? I give you my word of honor. Name a reasonable ransom and grant us parole, and I shall make it good."

"That is a greater courtesy than your cousin gave me," he said with a bitter twist of his mouth.

I snorted. "And what he paid me to give you into his custody was nowhere near what you paid. Neither Sir John nor I are landed, and James here nae yet knighted. But I can afford to pay a ransom—" I tilted my head toward Preston.

There was no reason to reveal our problems with Galloway to Sir Thomas. "I will guarantee payment for all three of us and the men-at-arms. You have the reputation of a reasonable man and I of an honorable one. I think we can agree on a price."

He named a ransom that would take all my profit for being sheriff. I winced at the amount, and Preston grumbled, but the sum was well worth it. Sir Thomas wrote out the pledge with his own hand, clear and legible, without needing a cleric to do it. We joined his servants in sleeping in the great hall wrapped in our cloaks, and the next morning, a purple stain creeping my forehead from the blow to my head, we rode toward Edinburgh. My stomach clenched with nerves at having to face the King and explain the embarrassing fact that I allowed us to be taken prisoner.

When we rode into Edinburgh, it was gone noontide the next day. I had a powerful urge to stop at the Sheep Heid Inn, get drunk as a scullion, and lie low. My duty, however, required that I inform my Lord King of the destruction of the band of reivers and my failure in allowing myself and my men to be taken prisoner by the English. Assuring Preston and James that the responsibility was mine, I allowed him and our men-at-arms to take our prisoner to the dungeon beneath the tolbooth. I handed over a few pennies to buy him a decent meal at the White Hart and proceeded to the castle. David had given me his trust in making me sheriff. I hoped this did not make him regret it.

In the great hall, His Grace was standing on the dais with Katherine and two men, maister craftsmen from their garb. One was pointing to something on a parchment. He still was eager to build a new tower, but planning for it had only begun.

When I stepped onto the dais and bowed, he waved the

craftsmen away, telling them to bring him a list of the buildings that would have to be torn down.

I waited until they were out of hearing before I told him my tale. He listened in silence to my report, his face emotionless except for a rush of color to the scar on his cheek. I delivered it without allowing my nervous twitches to show, and my voice was level and calm. I felt no better for his aloof mien. When I came to the end of the tale, there was silence.

He crossed his arms over his chest. "You come before me, having allowed my men to be taken prisoner, risking the truce. You do not expect me to be pleased."

"No, Your Grace. I do not."

'Have you any excuse for your capture?"

"It was a misjudgment, sire. That is the whole of it." I pulled myself to my full height, back straight and chin raised. "I was more concerned about ending the reivers and bringing one back for your justice than crossing the border."

Katherine laid her hand on his arm. "Pray you, dinnae be harsh with Sir Archibald. He put an end to the miscreants. Surely that is what you wanted."

The king's wide mouth pursed, and I wondered if he was recalling his own capture that had led to ten years of imprisonment by the English. "I do not commend misjudgments. But you returned with a miscreant to hang and the truce intact. And if you expect me to pay the ransom you incurred for you—" King David paused, but a corner of his mouth quirked. "—I shall do so." He patted her hand. "Since my lady speaks up for you."

I bent my head in thanks.

"Did the man reveal if someone was behind the attack?"

"He said he was merely a mosstrooper and claimed to only take orders. It was likely true. But he claimed that Fergus MacDowell had something to do with it, maybe even gave the orders."

"He was in Douglas territory, so he probably had Douglas's permission." He looked thoughtful. "Most of them being killed will have discouraged any more such alliances, though."

"Mayhap." I had never known Douglas to attack a monastery, but that did not mean he would never do so. "Or it could have been Angus. He has lands near the Nixon holdings and would dare such a thing. I dinnae believe the attack was merely to steal cattle, as you say. Killing so near to Edinburgh..." Frowning, I chewed my lip. "If they hadnae been caught, if one hadnae been hanged, would people have said that the King couldnae be trusted to keep peace in his own lands."

"And claim that Robert Stewart could do so." A muscle in David's jaw twitched. "Aye. I think you have the right to it. They arenae ready to defy me openly, but in secret? Aye. Angus would dare. He is a man who would dare much. So on the morrow, hold the sheriff's court. I want an end put to the reiver and all to see they can trust the king's justice."

"Aye, Your Grace." I considered thanking him for even considering paying the ransom, but it would sound like fawning. I made my obeisance and left. After that, I was more than ready for a large cup of wine.

CHAPTER SIX

The Next Day

My head was no longer throbbing from being skelpt in the fight, which cheered me up. I stopped at a street barber to have the four days of black stubble taken from my cheeks and had dressed to cut a dignified figure in my black surcoat with a crimson cloak fastened with an ornate silver clasp on my shoulder.

At the third hour after noon, the vaulted hall of the tolbooth was filled to overflowing. My weekly court was always crowded with litigants, witnesses, and the curious; the trial of a murderer had brought out everyone who could manage to cram their way in. My eyes lingered for a moment on five tumblers pressed against a wall in the crush. There were a few shouts and curses as the prisoner was dragged in, shackled hand and foot, and shoved in front of a low barrier that fenced off the onlookers.

The arrival of Abbot William of Newbattle, the prior, and a flock of senior monks, added to the entertainment. I greeted the abbot and called a chair to be placed next to the dais for him. His monks gathered behind him. I nodded, and the door was opened for the fifteen men of the jury to file in and sit around a table on the far side of the monks. I recognized several of them as burgesses I had seen around the city. My clerk of the court, a pudgy man who had failed at being a monk, waddled in with a writing box containing his parchment, ink and quills.

Rany stood staring at his feet, chains clanking as he shifted nervously, a man-at-arms on each side more to protect him than to keep him from escaping.

I sat in my chair in the middle of the dais. Gil, James, Walter Reed, Rauf of Herth, and half a score of men-at-arms were ranged around me. I wiped my damp palms on my thighs, hoping no one noticed. Acting as a judge still made my heart pound, but it was an important part of the duties of a sheriff.

My clerk huffed to the front of the dais and pronounced, "Rany of Peebles, you are accused of the unlawful slaying of two lay brothers at the Abbey of Newbattle and the theft of the abbey's cattle. How do you answer? Guilty or nae?"

Rany looked up, his Adam's apple bobbing as he gulped. "Guilty," he muttered, staring at me. "You ken I am guilty. You caught me yourself."

The jury looked disappointed since that left them with nothing to do, as this was our only trial on the day.

I stood. "Rauf of Peebles was taken in the midst of the crime of attacking an official of the King." However many men I had killed in battle, this was not a duty I enjoyed. "He is hereby sentenced to be hanged by the neck until dead. He is turned over to the constable of Edinburgh and on the morrow to be taken to Carlton Hill for execution. May God have mercy on his soul."

The onlookers cheered, a few shouting taunts at the prisoner as he was dragged through the rear door. The abbot made his way to me and gave me a solemn blessing.

On my stroll out of the tolbooth accompanied by Gil and

James, the puddles were frozen over, though the sky was clear, the winter sun giving little heat. A wain rumbled past and stopped down the street to deliver its load of faggots. As we walked, several merchants and a priest stopped to congratulate me on killing the band and condemning the miscreant. They seemed to credit me with returning safety to Edinburgh, as I watched the five minstrels were making their cheerful way to the White Hart. The woman with honey-colored eyes paused to look over her shoulder at me. Like most unmarried young women, she went bare-headed as an unmarried woman would, and her raven-colored hair flowed in waves down her back. She flashed me a smile, and her beauty left me breathless. Then one of the men tugged her arm to hurry her along.

Being near the tolbooth, the White Hart was a popular inn and well-run by the couple who owned it. The rushes were kept fresh, and they bought good wine from the ships that landed at Leith. Often prosperous merchants or a thirsty knight graced its board.

"That is done, and it made me thirsty," I said, veering to follow them. "I want a cup of wine."

Gil had an insolent grin. "Aye. You want wine."

I silently smiled at his teasing as we stepped into the stone building. A sign painted with a white deer, its horns spread wide, identified the tavern, and the wind streamed the smoke from its hearth northward from the thatch roof. A craftsman in a leather apron stood at the lowered shutters as someone handed him a mug. He tugged his forelock at me before hurrying away.

The inside of the tavern was long and narrow. Dark cross-beams stood on thick posts that marched to the end. The air had a smelled of woodsmoke, ale, and sweat. The short, stubby man with massive forearms stood on the right behind a wooden barrier that stretched across the room; behind it stood kegs of ale and wine. At the opposite end was a stone fireplace and a crackling fire. A potboy dodged between the tables carrying a platter with mugs of ale.

It was not quite time for dinner, but several onlookers from the trial had come over. The innkeeper, an apron tied around his waist, bustled out to me inside the doorway. "my lord Sheriff! Welcome!" He led to a table near the fire, shooing away the two men seated there and scrubbing the top with a cloth in his hand. "Our best table for you, my lord, right next to the fire."

"Bring us your best claret," I said, sinking down at the table. James and Gil took the other side. A moment later he hurried back, his potboy carrying a tray with a pottery flagon of wine and three pewter wine cups that he filled for us, bowing. I tasted it and nodded my approval.

The lutenist stood up from a nearby table, approached and bowed. "Sir Archibald," he said with a smoothly flowing French accent. "My brother, Estienne, wondered if it would be acceptable to make a song about your defeat of the thieves. We must add ballads about Scotland to those we brought with us from Poitiers."

I looked at the younger man at his elbow, who gave a small bow. Beside him, my golden-eyed girl flashed me a smile and my stomach twisted. "I havenae objection, though I doubt me that it is so noteworthy as to be a very fine ballad."

She had a rich voice with a laugh in it when she said, "Etienne can turn anything into a fine ballad, my lord." Speaking as much with her hands as her mouth, she continued, "If you would hear what he makes of it to be sure it does you credit, you may come to find us. We are staying in a small house on the next small street. You call it a close? Anyone will be telling where the lutenist and his family—"

The younger lassie, another sister, I thought, laughed behind her hand but had nothing to say.

"Cateline!" the lutenist exclaimed in French. "Do not be forward." He shook his head at me. "I apologize, my lord, for my sister. Of course, you would never call on a mere lutenist."

"Jaquet!" she replied, eyes flashing.

I stood. "I am nae so proud as all that." Sure I was blushing, but it did not show in the dim light. I gave a courteous bow of my head to Cateline, thrilled to have at last learned her name. "Mademoiselle, I would be pleased to hear your brother's ballad."

She darted a triumphant look at her brother as she curtsied in reply, her azure cotehardie pooling around her feet. The lutenist shook his head again, but only said, "I thank you for your courtesy, my lord." With a scolding look, he picked up their jar of ale and shepherded his family out the door.

Gil was chortling when I sat back down, so I kicked him. It just made him laugh harder and James joined in. Then I had to laugh as well. "Och, I am nae monk, you ken."

James nodded. "Aye. That is one bonnie woman. That she is."

I nodded, but Gil shook his head. "I like a bit more meat on my woman's bones." He wiggled his eyebrows. "There is a lassie in the kitchen I have my eye on."

"Good for you, Gil. You deserve one." Thoughtfully sipping my wine, it seemed to me that we both deserved some peace, enjoyment, even love and pleasure if we could find it. Perhaps I might find exactly that if in a few days, I paid a visit to the lutenist and his beautiful sister.

"Sadly, the taxes are still waiting for me to be calculated at the castle." I dropped a handful of coins on the table. "But you both did a braw job catching our reivers, so enjoy yourselves whilst you can."

John Allincrum, a portly man, clad in a resplendent red cotehardie with a mustard-colored cloak and matching chaperon for a hat, bustled toward me. "It is all the talk of the burgh that you have made the roads once more safe for trade. A wise choice that King Davie, God keep His Grace, gave you the position."

I nodded to the head of the silversmith's guild, who had crafted the hilt of the claymore I carried. "No more than my duty, Maister Allincrum. The King expects the roads to be safe, as do I. And never will I stand by while a monastery is attacked."

"That is braw to hear. And I hope you will look into the neglect of the city walls as well." He shook his head, the elaborate drape of his chaperon flapping. "They have been sorely neglected of late."

I kept from rolling my eyes. Of course, there would be a complaint to match the praise. I had already learned that the burgesses were never satisfied with what their taxes paid for. But of course, he might have some reason, so I said, "If you have concerns about the walls, bring them to me. My door is always open to you or any guildmaister." No doubt more complaints would wait for me in my chambers.

CHAPTER SEVEN

The Next Morning

I itched to call on the minstrels to see Cateline once more. I pictured the gleam of her amber eyes, a dimple that formed in her cheek when she smiled. But calling on them so soon would be overeager and undignified. The last thing I wanted was for her to despise me. So I spent the day going over the tedious accounts of the taxes and depositing them in the heavy, iron-bound kist with two large locks. I received 200 merks per year, much more than my cousin had ever given me. More than one sheriff had helped themselves to more, but David knew I would not. And my rightful sum was more riches than I had ever expected to have, though I had done well in jousting. I bought a small locked kist that was soon heavy with the spoils.

On the fourth day after the trial, after morning mass, I fretted about what to wear, as though a change of clothes would make me more fair of face.

Gil lost patience and pushed my arms into a blue doublet and settled my fur-lined, green cloak on my shoulders. "It is time you were nae pining." He urged me toward the door.

With a nod, I set Gil free for the afternoon. From his grin

as he hurried in leaving, I suspected his impatience was that I was keeping him from the kitchen lassie who had him enthralled.

I set off, followed by two men-at-arms, down the curving road toward the base of Castle Rock and the burgh proper. The streets were busy with wains carrying goods, servants with baskets scurrying to buy food for dinner, half a score of Knights Hospitallers clopped past, a red cross emblazoned on their gleaming white surcoats and cloaks. According to the seneschal, the musician's lodging was down a vennel just past the White Hart. I stopped at a farrier's stable, told my men to await me at the inn next door, and strode to turn into the vennel. It was shady in the narrow confines between two buildings.

Two wee lasses sat cross-legged, chanting a rhyme as they clapped each other's hands. An older lad threw a stick for a shaggy-coated mutt. The shutters of the next house were shut, but the sounds of voices and a harp spilled into the morning.

I followed the sounds and knocked. A minstrel I did not recognize opened the door and stumbled back, hands raised. His eyes were wide. "What—" He stared at my sword. "Whatever you want, sir. Just say."

Cateline appeared at his shoulder. " Oh là! It is the Lord Sheriff! Do not be a ninny." She swept me a curtsy, her slightly worn, yellow silk dress pooling around her feet and her dark hair flowing down her back in soft waves.

Offering my hand to raise her, I inclined my head in greeting. "Demoiselle."

The greeter stood aside. The room was crowded with musicians. A man with a vielle was tuning his instrument while one of Cateline's brother held his flute and argued with a man holding a tabor over the correct beat of a passage. Beyond them, her younger sister and another woman had their heads together, humming a tune with a look of concentration on their faces.

"Ave, Sir Archibald," called the lutenist, who was standing with a harpist next to the hearth where a small fire crackled. "Welcome to our humble abode."

They all left off what they had been doing to watch as I made my past them. I asked, "These arenae all family, or it has grown most quickly."

"We share the house with fellow minstrels and can afford better than alone until there is better weather for travel. And it is the chance to learn while we wait for the traveling season. My friend is teaching me a Scottish melody and I will teach him some French." He gestured to the red-haired harpist who was holding a gleaming clàrsach harp and the yellow-dyed shirt of a Highlander with tightly fitted green hose. "You will listen, Sir Archibald, and tell me if I have it correctly?"

The Highlander huffed. "I am the one who would ken that, man."

Smiling, I nodded at the comment as Cateline put a cup of wine in my hand. "I havenae doubt of that. But I would happily be your audience if it might aid you."

The brother carrying his flute and looking abashed, said, "I fear I have failed so far at a ballad, my lord, but I have not given up."

Waving the matter away, I said, "If you would like a song with a jest in it, mayhap, Sir William Ramsay will tell you the tale of how he tricked the English into letting me go." I chuckled and shook my head at the memory. "But that reminds me, Will has gone to fetch his bride to Edinburgh for their wedding and I mean to remind him that he was impressed with your singing at the king's feast."

"That would be most welcome, sir." Jacquet used his foot to push a three-legged stool to me. "Forgive that we have no chair to offer you, but sit yourself down, please. I shall play. Cateline shall sing."

Cateline motioned to her sister. "Perrette, sing with me."

They launched into *I long for Thy Virginitie*. The wistful sound and words and the words went through me. My hands ached to touch her.

The other musicians must have stopped what they were doing for when it ended, the lutenist said, "Well played!" and the others briefly applauded.

The harpist nodded with a satisfied look. "Now I would learn *Douce Dame Jolie*. It would sound excellent, I think me, on the harp."

"Brawly done!" I stood. "I shall certainly recommend you to Will Ramsay." I set down the wine upon a small table piled with paper scribbled with song lyrics and took Cateline's hand to tuck into the bend of my arm. "Demoiselle, will you see me to the door?"

Her eyes crinkled in amusement, no doubt because it was only a few steps, and she ducked her head. "Certainly, my lord."

At the door, I bent so that I could whisper in her ear. "I would meet you again. If you would want to, that is. To speak —more privily."

Her lips twitched as though she were suppressing a smile. "Tomorrow I will attend morning mass at Saint Giles. You might find me there."

The next morning, I left Gil with the horses and slipped into the nave of Saint Giles Kirk. Cateline was next to the rear arch. I waited, quietly making the responses, until the priest gave the dismissal. " Ite, missa est."

"Deo gratias," I murmured and watched as she waved

away her brothers and sister, motioning toward the apse where the shrine of the Blessed Mother was located. Once they were out the doors, I too entered the apse where she knelt, her head bowed and covered by a gossamer veil. I crossed myself and lit a candle.

Cateline also crossed herself and stood facing me. "I hoped you would come," she said, speaking French.

I took her hand and turned it to kiss her palm. "You should have known I could not stay away."

"Come." Holding my hand, she had me follow her out of the church and around to the rear of the kirkyard.

Robins were chirping in the dense pines. I leaned back against a thick trunk, holding her hand, and drank in her face. "Cateline. A name nearly as lovely as you."

She flickered a smile. "I am named after my grandmother."

She leaned against me and I wrapped my arm around her. "Does she live?" Desire flashed through me like fire.

"No. She lived in Calais and my father went to take her away." She grimaced. "Both died in the English slaughter."

"Ah. And that is why you came to Scotland instead of England." I pushed back her veil and kissed her forehead.

"You Scots do love music. We have done well enough, but... It is not home."

"Give it time. You have already made friends. The other minstrels." I rubbed my cheek against her raven-dark hair and breathed in the scent of rose petals. "And me."

She laughed. "La. You men. I know what you want."

"I do. What man would not?" I was consumed by it, but I had to chuckle. "I am no better than the rest of them. But I will help you and your family. And I will take naught that isnae freely offered."

She bent her head back, looking up into my face. "I would feel safe with you."

I kissed her, softly at first, then when her lips parted, hungrily. "If I send Gil for you, will you join me for supper?"

"Only supper?"

I stroked my fingers down her soft neck. "I might hope for more."

CHAPTER EIGHT

Gil waved as he rode out of the bailey as sputters of snow flurries drifted on the wind. When he was through the upper gate, I went back into the keep and paced. Then I smoothed my hands down my blue wool doublet, checked my pointed leather shoes to be sure they were not scuffed and rubbed my chin to check for stubble. I paced some more.

A squire in the royal livery hurried toward me. "Sir Archibald, His Grace requires you."

"Now?" I asked and then realized it was absurd. Of course, now. A royal summons was always now.

To my relief, the door banged open ahead of a brisk wind, carrying a scent of snow along with Cateline and Gil. She shook snow from her cloak and turned to thank Gil for his escort.

I took her hand, kissed it, and tucked it into my elbow. "Lead the way, lad." With her beside me, I followed him up the stairs and into a room with air heavy with smells of the oak fire, lavender, and damp furs, filled with men in the king's following awaiting his desires. Sir John Preston nodded to me. Walter Haliburton, John Herries, and others sat or stood about, playing cards and discussing when the weather would be good enough for riding after the deer.

"Archie!" Will exclaimed. "I was about to seek you since I've already paid my respects to the king." He clapped me on the shoulder and grinned. "And a fair lass." He inclined his head courteously. "One with a very bonnie voice, as I recall me."

Smiling, Cateline curtsied. "my lord. That is most kind of you to say."

"You recall correctly. I have never heard a finer voice. But where is your affianced? Is the countess nae with you?"

"She is resting at the house we have taken in the town." He chuckled. "And insisted that she couldnae see the King until she has unpacked her finest kirtle and gown."

I thumped him on the arm. "We will talk later. I cannae keep His Grace waiting."

When I turned to follow the waiting page, Cateline tugged on my arm. "You cannot mean to take me in with you to see the king," she said in French. A line had appeared between her plucked brows.

"I mean to do exactly that." My mouth twitched. "His Grace never objects to the sight of a beautiful woman. Besides, it might be to your benefit for him to be reminded that he enjoyed your singing. He does not send a purse to every minstrel who comes before him."

The page opened the door to the next chamber.

A dozen courtiers and servants in the royal livery stood around the room, filling the room with a low murmur of conversation. A fire burned on the hearth, and next to it, King David and Katherine Mortimer sat at a table draped with an oriental carpet, a chess game in play. Katherine picked up a carved ivory knight and tapped it to her lips, pondering her next move. Standing beside the king, watching with a smile, was the white-haired William de Landallis,

Bishop of Saint Andrews. On the other side of the room, eyes narrowed, the hulking Earl of Angus watched them.

The page whispered something to the king, and the game paused. I bowed low.

"Sir Archibald." The King swept a look of admiration over Cateline. "And a bonnie companion."

She swept a low curtsy to the ground and gracefully rose.

"The minstrel who sang so beautifully for us." Katherine's smile at me was both amused and knowing. "And I think Sir Archibald enjoyed it as well."

"I did, my lady. Very much." It was best to err on the side of courtesy to the king's leman. Looking to the king, I said, "You wanted me, Your Grace."

"Aye. Her Grace has received permission to visit her mother in England. I want you to arrange an appropriate escort for her. Percy is supposed to be waiting at the Tweed to see her safely to Hertford Castle."

Katherine looked down to study the chessboard, a tiny smile playing about her lips. Silence fell across the room like a blanket.

"Shall I lead them myself, Sire?"

"You are needed here, Archie." He stroked his chin. "Have Preston lead them with a score of other knights. Twoscore men-at-arms should be sufficient."

In the silence, Angus motioned to a servant and whispered something.

For a moment, I was speechless, not that I could blame the lady or even the king, though he could have been kinder. Their marriage had never seemed happy, joined together when they were still bairns. "When does Her Grace want to depart?"

"In three days. That gives you enough time to arrange her escort—" He smiled at Cateline. "—and still have ample time to give the bonnie lass a tour of the keep."

Thus dismissed, I retreated from the chamber, Cateline grasping my arm. I spotted John Preston, pulled him aside, and explained that he would lead the queen's escort.

"Aye," Preston said, nodding. "I ken the best men for the job. We need to make a good show or else give insult."

Nodding to Preston, I took Cateline's hand. "Hie before someone else wants something." We hurried up a flight of stairs, threw back her head, and laughed as we went. I closed the door firmly behind us.

All my papers had been shoved aside to make room for a flagon of wine and two pewter wine goblets. I poured us each a cup. Our hands brushed when I handed her one, and the touch sent heat through me like the warmest day of summer.

"The town is abuzz about the king's leman. She is lovely, but..." She frowned, sipping the wine. "They also say he needs an heir. Surely that is no way to get one."

"Poor Queen Joanna has nae given him one in these thirty years." Everyone said the blame was hers, but it had been noticed that his mistresses had no children either. "I think they have given up. So he looks elsewhere."

"But a bastard could not be his heir." Her eyes widened. "Archie... I..."

I chuckled. "The word doesnae offend me. If the queen became a religious, the King might succeed in a divorce. And Katherine is unmarried." I put down my wine and stroked her silk-covered arm. "Surely we have better things to talk of than the queen. Tell me more about how you came to grace Scotland with that beautiful voice."

She wrinkled her nose. "I am not sure I would have been eager if I had known how very much it rains here. But Jaquet's oldest friend is a first mate on a cog that sails from La Rochelle." She shook her head. "You do not want to hear me go on about that. I would rather hear how you came to be so trusted by the king."

"We grew up together in France." I savored for a moment that this beautiful, talented women was here in my chamber, then with a gentle touch wrapped my arms around her and pulled her closer.

She looked up at me, lifting a hand to cup my jaw, amber eyes glowing in the candlelight. "You know that was quite magnificent in the tolbooth. All those men obeying your every word and you bringing justice for the poor, slain monks. I am glad I was there to see it."

I bent and kissed the narrow bridge of her nose. "I am glad you were there that I finally found you. I had sought you since the night of the feast." I brushed my lips against her silky cheek. She trembled, and I drew her against me to enjoy the warmth of her flesh, my fingers tangling in the raven fall of her hair. I bent to kiss her. Her arms slid around me, and she leaned into my embrace, her breath coming as fast as mine. I kissed her eyelids, stroked the warm, soft flesh beneath the neck of her kirtle. My body quickened with need.

Once more, I took her mouth with mine. A log in the fireplace collapsed with a shower of sparks as I lifted her into my arms. Her arms encircled my neck as she nestled against me, and I carried her into the bedchamber and lowered her onto the bed.

Our fevered hands tore away clothes to find eager flesh beneath our hands, stroking and exploring. When I buried myself inside her, she rose to meet me. We moved slowly at first, finding our tempo and then faster. I met the urgent rhythms of her body, and her warm breath mingled with mine.

Afterward, I lay on my back, her head nestled on my shoulder, wrapped a strand of her long hair around my fingers, and kissed the top of her head. I listened to the sounds of the castle. The bell of Saint Margaret's Kirk rang for vespers and nearer, the footfall of a guard in the hallway. I ran my hand down her back and over the soft swell of her buttocks, breathing in her rose perfume mixed with the tang of sex.

After a time, she shifted and playfully tugged at the hair on my chest. "You promised me supper."

I laughed, running my hand up her arm. "Aye. But how could I think of food with you in my arms?"

She propped herself up on her elbow, the fall of her hair around us like a curtain. "The songs say we could live on love and have no need for food."

"We could try. It might be true." I caught her to me, pulling her down to my kiss. This time when we came together, it was slow and soft, as though it might last forever.

CHAPTER NINE

December 1359

December 1359

The next months were busy. When she was not practicing or singing with her brothers and sister, Cateline was with me. I leased a house for her, and her siblings were often there, music spilling into the street. But underneath was a growing tension.

The next month, there was an audit of the royal exchequer. It was plain that several of the earls, Douglas, March, Angus, and Stewart, David's heir, were appropriating taxes from their holdings that should have come to the crown. The sums from their lands were laughably small. The payment from Douglas's Peeblesshire was a ludicrous 16 merks. Several lords in Galloway, MacDowell, Agnew McCulloch, and Adair, had refused to pay any taxes at all, claiming their princedom owed nothing to the King of the Scots. I ground my teeth and slammed my fist on the table.

The payment of 10,000 pounds English for this year was barely scraped together and made at Berwick-upon-Tweed. Making it the next year would be impossible, nor would it leave funds for the king's household or for running the government. If the pope had not allowed the King to use half the church tithes for the year, it would not have been made, but the pope had given permission to use part of the church tithes for only this year.

The King was convinced that they meant to make it impossible to make the payment the following year, and he would be honor bound to return to imprisonment in England. In a rage, he dashed a cup of wine against the wall and bellowed that he would never let that happen. If he were imprisoned again, Stewart would see that he was never released and, in effect, would rule as guardian until David died in an English dungeon. The King now had a following of hundreds of knights and minor lords, but we knew we did not have enough to defeat our own earls.

Convinced that the only solution for the ominous threat was to renegotiate the treaty for his release, he wrote to his good brother, King Edward, that they urgently needed to meet. In November, Edward agreed to meet in London to discuss how the treaty might be changed, so we prepared to ride south with safe conduct in hand. Thomas, Earl of Mar, rode in with a retinue of thirty men-at-arms to accompany us.

Cateline walked with me to the bailey yard. "I am sorry, Cateline." I laid my hand on her belly and felt the bairn move. Five months gone, she was even more beautiful than ever. Looking at her took my breath away; being with child had only made her more beautiful. "I will return well before your time."

"You are the Sheriff of Lothian and the king's man. Such things must be, I ken. But take a care, my love, in England and return to me and your son soon."

Happiness went through me like a warm flood. "Are you so certain it is a lad?"

"You would hardly believe the kicks he gives me already."

She squeezed my hand. "No girl could kick so fiercely, I am sure of it."

I squeezed her hand in response, and I left her with a kiss and a purse of silver in case she had any need while I was gone. Herries would be my depute while I was gone and stood by watching the chaos of the bailey.

I led a hundred men-at-arms, and twenty knights accompanying the King were mounting, tack clacking, and horses snorting or stomping. A dozen horse boys led out our spare mounts. Servants loaded sumpters with packs of clothes, supplies, and even bedding.

Lady Katherine walked the King to his mount. He kissed her mouth and swung into the saddle. The rest of us formed up, the royal lion rampant banner waving overhead as we took the steep, bending road to Edinburgh. There were a few cheers as we left but many puzzled looks and frowns at the news of the King returning to England. I also had serious doubts, but David had growled angrily when I told him so. I kept quiet on my thoughts that King Edward was no solution to our problems.

The sun was a misty gold high in the winter sky as we rode through the gate and turned south. We were in luck that the coastal route was dry, and we made good time to the River Tweed.

When we gained the far bank, a flock of crows burst from the dry bracken. "They are telling us we had better hie home as soon as may be." I did not believe in omens, but they made my skin crawl even so.

"Aye, I didnae expect to be back in England so soon," Sir John Preston said. "And the sooner back in Scotland, the better."

"We will bring good news with the good God's help." He signaled to proceed ahead. "Sir Thomas kens to expect us at

Norham Castle. Let us reach it so we can leave at first light in the morn."

The next day, after a ride stopping only briefly to rest our mounts, we reached Henry Percy's Tynemouth Castle and its priory on a rocky headland overlooking the sea, crashing on sharp, craggy boulders. The baron's steward was none too friendly, but reluctantly allowed us shelter for the night. Crossing the Tyle by ferry was slow, and the ferrymen scowled and muttered about Goddammed Scots, although they were paid well. We passed peddlers and pilgrims who scrambled off the road at the sight of us, and workers in the fields stared at us in alarm, ready to run. Many fled into the woods.

The bells of nones were ringing when we reached Durham, its towering cathedral and vast castle crowning the ridge above the twisting River Wear, and the castle reluctantly gave us shelter at King Edward's command, some guards muttering curses and not bothering to hide it.

We rode past golden fields being seeded with a winter crop. Children ran, waving their arms to scare off marauding birds. A peregrine soared overhead, looking for prey. A dog dodged into a verge, carrying a hare in its mouth. But everywhere, anyone who could evade us did, dodging out of sight or, if they could not, eyeing the wind-ruffled Lion Rampant banner with hate.

The scowls bothered Mar not at all. He beamed at sights familiar to him and pointed them out. He had not made it to France with most of the young nobles, but had been seized by the English and raised there. Apparently, William Carsewell, who had reared him in England, had treated him well, for he seemed happy to be back. He chuckled at memories the sights brought back to him and assured me that I would grow to like the place as well as he did. I doubted that. Preston reminisced less happily about months in the Tower of London.

Since we had left Durham, the roads to and from London were being patrolled, and we eventually came to some hardened professionals. I had fought such men in Scotland, their faces leathered by the sun and wind. Most were away fighting the French, but Edward must not trust his own people not to rebel against their heavy taxes for him to have kept some here. They were stationed at a bridge and calmly lowered their pikes and raised their crossbows, blocking the way. The serjeant-at-arms examined the royal seal I handed him, the King looking slightly amused.

At the King's command, I gave them some silver for drinks for their courtesy, and we were allowed to cross and continue on our way. Sometimes we passed groups of travelers bundled against the cold, merchants, monks, hawkers, and peddlers. They gave way to such an armed band of knights, but so far from the border, they no longer looked at us as though we were devils come to steal, if not their souls, then certainly their food and burn their houses over their heads.

Our journey continued for a week through woods and copses of oak, juniper, beechwood, and willows thick along the rivers, full of the sounds of birds and foxes and their prey rustling in the undergrowth. Sometimes the forest was so thick that their bare branches arched over our heads. The valleys were patchworks of brown fields around villages of wattle-and-daub hovels surrounding a walled tower house of their lord.

I had never been nearly so far into England, so I watched all the changing scenes as we rode, but frankly, it was not so different from much of France and far less beautiful than Scotland. I decided not to mention my opinion to the Earl of Mar. After seven days, I was sore and bored. It had been a long time since I had spent so day after day in the saddle. My back ached, and my arse hurt. Everyone was grumbling when we stopped for the night. Eventually, the land leveled out. Mar said we were finally nearing London, and our stay at a small keep would be the last outside London. The King nodded thoughtfully.

Even in the morning, the stench of London reached us before the walls even came into sight, a stink of the river, smoke from countless chimneys, slaughter yards, and the piss, shit, and sweat of thousands and thousands of people. London had spilled through the gates so that hovels and even shops sprawled beside the road filled with peddlers trundling barrows of goods, others piled with vegetables, women carrying baskets of eggs or chickens and geese under their arms beneath a sun dimmed by a layer of smoke.

The guards at the gate had had word of our coming, and we were met by threescore men-at-arms led by two men in polished armor too elaborate to have ever seen battle.

The older half-bowed from the saddle to King David. "Sir Symond de Benyngton—" he seemed to choke on the next words. "—Your Grace. Sheriff of London and my fellow sheriff, Sir John de Chichester." The younger, rather muscular man made a slight obeisance. "The escort will see to your safety through London in case there are—" he coughed. "—protests or violence. That would be for the best if you would be sure your men do not retaliate if any objects are thrown."

Sir John said, "Few know of your arrival, so there should be few problems. You are expected at Blackfriars Abbey, of course."

I kept my face straight at the idea that we needed protection from a much smaller number of English men-at-arms, but it would doubtless be less than diplomatic to slaughter the peasants of London before asking King Edward for a favor. So the mail-clad men-at-arms took places spaced out beside us, and a serjeant-at-arms flanked by a couple of his pike-wielding men led out bellowing for the people to make way but not announcing for whom. Our armies had never reached even nearly this far south, so we were not hated with the same passion as in the north, but that did not mean they would not try to kill us given a chance. I rode with my hand on the hilt of my sword. David shook his head at me, but I just shrugged. A few rocks were thrown our way, but mostly the people were more interested in not being trampled under our hooves than throwing things at us.

The King pointed toward the Tower of London visible above the houses in the distance, but soon the sight was cut off by the overhanging upper stories of the houses. I rode carefully to avoid the filth slopping from the sewer along the side of the street. Boys ran beside our entourage, hooting and shouting insults. Women stuck their heads through the windows. One yelled curses after us, but most just looked curious.

At last, the walls of Blackfriars Abbey rose before us. The porter opened the gate before the serjeant had finished bellowing his command to do so, and we filed in the King and Earl of Mar in the lead. I took a deep breath of relief as the cool of the garden washed over me. Large yews and hazels stood guard in the middle of the garden's dead grass.

The abbot, silk habit shimmering in the sunshine, stood in the middle of the extensive garden, a covey of monks in white habits behind him. He stretched out his hands in greeting. "Your Grace, most puissant lords, welcome be you, by God's grace!"

King David urged his horse forward a few steps and dismounted before the abbot. "God be here, Father Abbot! And good day to you if you have refreshments and beds for us."

While they exchanged the usual courtesies, I climbed stiffly from the saddle. More in need of sustenance and a bed than courtesies, I was hoping we were in time for supper as it was not yet compline. Lay brothers were scurrying to lead our mounts to the stables, and the guest maister was frantically signaling for the men-at-arms to be taken to a lesser guest hall up the stairway where they would no doubt be crowded into a long chamber to share, but hopefully, there would be room for the knights in the guest hall proper. Servants were piling bags on the ground from the sumpters. There was no telling how long it would take for the right bags to find their way to their owners.

I jerked my head to the serjeant and told him to find two men-at-arms to be placed outside the king's door. The abbot urged the King and earl toward the chamber reserved for the highest of degree while the guest maister clucked around us like a mother duck trying to herd the knights to the guest hall, assuring us that we could make our ablutions before we were made welcome in the refectory for supper.

I followed into the long hallway, where doors opened off on each side. Apparently, we would only have to share two to a room, so I grabbed James's arm and told him he could share with me, even though he was not yet a knight. At least we could scrub the dirt of the road from our hands and faces before the bell rang to summon us to our supper.

The room was filled with long trestle tables and a dais at the head where a monk sat behind a podium. We gratefully piled onto the benches at a table to one side the guest maister pointed us toward.

Baskets of bread, fresh butter, and large bowls of fish pottage, redolent with leeks and thyme, were brought. The monk on the podium intoned an excessively long prayer, but at last, we could fall.

"My belly was about to meet my backbone," James muttered between bites.

I decided I could be excused from attending compline until I had clean and presentable clothing to wear. Most seemed to agree with me because a stream of knights flowed back to the guesthouse. Without bothering with the rush-light, James and I shed our armor and sought our bed, barely wide enough for us, but neither of us was awake long enough to complain.

The next day was chaos as the English King, his advisers, and their entourage arrived. Of course, they had considered that they had to have a larger entourage than King David, so the men-at-arms must be double our own. They lined the walls of the priory and the way to the huge, upper frater.

The English King walked past without looking my way. He had not changed a much since I last saw him at Roxburgh Castle, though his carefully combed hair and beard were grayer, and his belly hung a little over his gold-studded belt. A bishop in a gold brocade gown and an enormous pectoral cross dangling on a gold chain carried a gold pastoral staff. He seemed a hearty enough fellow that he would be weighed down by all that gold.

I went to guard the door as David entered, winking happily at me as he passed, saw that the guards were in their places beside the doors, and left them to it. I had been relieved not to be inside for the negotiations since King Edward had good reason to have no friendly feelings toward me. He had a wonderful memory for a grudge. Not knowing how the negotiations were proceeding was less comfortable. Thinking about what David might propose, that he might once again propose to make an English prince his heir, made my stomach cramp, so I did my best not to think about it.

Having no prospect of work that morning, I suggested to Preston that we make a tour of the city. I had donned a clean doublet and hose and tucked a bag of silver in my scrip for our entertainment. I rubbed my chin and resolved to find a barber. James was happy to come along with us, and an English knight who introduced himself as Sir Geoffrey Hendy even attached himself to us saying he had nothing better to do until his duties after compline, so we strolled out of Blackfriars Abbey and went to gawk at Saint Paul's Cathedral with its high, pointed arches and windows and its spire so lofty that I had to crane my neck back to see the top. We left staring at the cathedral to walk along Fleet Street with stalls along the side of the road and some impressive churches. Lawyers in red, blue, and green robes and bell-shaped hats streamed out of a church that had been turned over for their use. When I asked Sir Geoffrey about another church, its doorways flanked by columns and topped with concentric circles, he said it was the Church of Saint Bride, founded by the saint her own self. I insisted we stop so I could light a candle to the patron saint of all Douglas ilk for Cateline's safe delivery. Visiting London did not make up for how much I missed her.

James pointed out that our entertainment had been a bit godly, so we trailed through some alleys where coal boys, water-sellers, and prostitutes pursued their trades until we came to a tavern where Sir Geoffrey said the pies and chops were mouthwatering. We secured a table and asked the blowsy-haired server what was best in the kitchen. Beef and kidney pies, a platter piled with mutton chops, and bowls of buttered turnips and cabbage were soon laid before us and soon emptied. The ale was excellent with a rich, toasty taste, but I could not take a chance to have a muzzy head in the middle of so many Englishers, so I drank sparingly. I did have a second slice of the pie that was dripping with gravy.

The shadows were lengthening in the late afternoon as we strolled toward the abbey. I stopped at the open-fronted stall of a barber who shaved my cheeks and trimmed my short beard to a point with consummate skill as he gossiped about the goings on of the King negotiating with Scots and that the Black Prince would soon make a truce with the French. He shook his head over it, sure that the prince could defeat them with ease if only the King would let him. Seeing how good his shave was, the others lined up for his ministrations. Replete with food and feeling well-groomed, we reached the abbey. The compline bell was ringing, so our new friend went to his duties while we joined the stream going into the church, the King leading the way. The Earl of Mar was nowhere in sight.

We streamed into the refectory for supper as soon as the service was over. Of course, the King joined the prior to eat in the prior's house.

Sir John Herries glanced around to see who was nearby. "I was guarding the door when the day's negotiations ended." He made a dramatic pause. "If the King's look had been a blade, Mar would be dead."

I paused, my cup of ale halfway to my mouth, but I had not decided whether I wanted to pursue the comment when James leaned toward Sir John and whispered, "Do you ken why?"

"He is always in debt, even worse now than ever." I grimaced. "And is fonder of the English than I like."

"Aye, and King Edward was smirking as he left, like a cat in the cream."

I shook my head. The English King being satisfied had never been good news for Scotland.

The next day to break the boredom, for there was little for us to do inside the heavily guarded walls of the abbey, Sir John proposed a trip by boat to see the Tower of London. "From outwith its walls," he said with a laugh. There were stairs on the south side of the abbey down to where boats were moored. I hired a rowboat to take us to the Tower. Oars stirred and rippled the stinking black water of the Thames. The huge tower within its moat was as grim as I had expected, but we found a tavern with decent ale to while away the time.

I refused to consider another journey by boat, but James begged to see where the hero William Wallace was executed. It was a longish walk. The place stunk of cow and sheep shit, and the bawling of animals about to be slaughtered filled the air. The only sign of where Wallace had died was a scaffold where three bodies hung, and ravens darted to pick at their eyes. We stopped by the Church of Saint Bartholomew the Great and lit candles for his soul.

At supper that night, I could not help myself and sighed noisily. "How long do you think they will take? I can live without walking another step in the filth." I had seen as much of London as I cared to. But no one knew what was being said within the chambers where the two kings were meeting, only that King Edward still looked smug when he left. The Earl of Mar no longer took part. Every time I saw David, he was beaming. He had proposed in the past to name one of the English princes as his heir if he had no heir of his body. It had nearly caused riots. He hated Robert Stewart, which I could not fault, but Scots would never accept an English heir or, God's mercy upon us, an English king.

After two more days of boredom, the negotiations were finally over. We rode back to Scotland with a grinning King who refused to say what had been decided. He promised to reveal everything once we reached Scone, where the King had called a council meeting of all the great magnates before we left Scotland. I accepted it on the first day but had to speak up on the second.

As I rode beside him, I braced myself, sure he would not take my opinion kindly. "Your Grace..."

He turned his head, eyebrow raised.

"To name one of the princes as your heir. They willnae accept it—the Parliament." I wanted to shout at him or shake sense into him. Looking straight ahead, I fought to keep my voice calm, but it came out a growl. "How could you be so—"

I bit off the word. Even from me, calling him a fool was too far.

"My heir will be my own son."

I jerked my head to look at him. "With your wife remaining in England? Only God can perform Immaculate Conception!"

His face flooded with color, and he ground his teeth. Through clenched lips, he said, "Dinnae go too far, Archie."

I tilted my head in acknowledgment. "Sire, I will support you with my life, but I do nae want either of our lives wasted in a rebellion. How can you convince them you will have an heir? The parliament will never agree to an English heir. I was there when they swore to that."

Riding silently for a minute, then he shrugged. "It willnae be a secret for long. My wife is entering a monastery. She told me she intends to take vows. It willnae be immediately, but soon. There are plans to be made, and she needs her brother's permission. But once she has taken her vows, I will appeal to the pope for a divorce."

I blinked and stared at the King, unable to hide my astonishment.

Mar's horse, directly behind us, snorted and sidled. When I looked over my shoulder, he was bringing the animal under control. "Foot slipped and spurred him."

"Will he give a divorce for that?" I asked.

"Bishop Bishop de Landallis believes he will." The King smiled, his eyes sparkling. "I will marry Katherine as soon as I am free. I hope no bairn is born before, but he can be declared legitimate, should that happen."

"That is..." I scratched my chin. "That is much to take in." I took a deep breath. I was sure he needed to hear something that he would not welcome. "But even so, you willnae convince the lords to agree. Robert Stewart will fight it, and so will my cousin."

"It is merely a way to convince the English to wait for the ransom. Of course, I wouldnae agree to an English king. But the ransom? We cannae pay! Then when I have an heir, it will be too late for the English to object." He patted his horse's neck. "I think you are wrong and that they will see the sense in my plan. No one wants Scotland impoverished. And with the truce, the English are now negotiating with the French. They could easily turn their armies our way. That must be prevented at all costs."

The ransom for the French king, taken prisoner at the Battle of Poitiers, would be even larger than the crippling ransom for David, and word was there would be a truce between the two kingdoms. But after the years of war, after the destruction of Burnt Candlemas... There were too many dead and suffering to save Scotland from the English, to risk it now on a bairn who had not been born. Nor could we assume what would happen in the negotiations between the English and the French. But my argument seemed to only stiffen his resolve.

CHAPTER TEN

January 1360, Scone Palace

William de Landallis, Bishop of Saint Andrews, wearing his tall miter and carrying his gilt shepherd's crook, walked beside the king. Along with Will and Sir John and half a dozen other knights, I followed them. James brought up the rear. At the end of the long enfilade of stuffy chambers, a guard opened the rear door of the great hall so we could step onto the dais. Waves of conflicting smells of sweat, musk, and lavender wafted in the air.

I barely had time to pick out the familiar faces amongst the hundred or more men standing at the benches ranked before the dais, men I had grown up with, fought with or beside, or briefly met at court. Herries nodded to me, and Alexander Haliburton met my eyes with a smile. The murmur of conversation stopped as they rose, all eyes on David. Most looked on impassively, a few smiled, and a handful scowled.

The bishop raised his hands and intoned a prayer for God to guide the kingdom's rulers. The King sat in the throne-like chair. He leaned forward. "As you all ken, I bring news of a new agreement with Edward of England to ease the burden of my ransom. We all ken it has been crippling our finances. The debt is more than we can pay—" He turned his gaze first to Douglas and then to Strathearn. "—after the losses and damage of the long war. So my good-brother has agreed that if I grant the Earldom of Moray to the great Knight of the Garter, Henry de Grossmont, Earl of Lancaster, Steward of England, and failing to his daughter and her heir to be held as freely as by—"

Patrick of Dunbar leapt to his feet. "That earldom is mine!"

Douglas rose a few places across from Dunbar, his face clamped like a fist. "God's blood!" he exploded. "John of Gaunt is marrying the Lancaster's daughter. You mean to give Moray to him!" He turned to Robert Stewart. "What say you to this treachery, Robert?"

I looked toward Will, his face tight with alarm. None of us carried any more than a dagger in a council. I stepped closer to David, blood rushing in my ears.

In the rising cacophony of voices, Robert Stewart yelled, "He is trying to cheat me out of my inheritance!" He shook his fist at the king. "You would name that whoreson John of Gaunt as heir."

His ruddy face flushed even redder than usual, John Menteith growled, "Time to teach you a lesson."

I stepped to stand beside the King between him and the Stewart. Blood pounded in my ears.

The King rose to his feet, his face pale with fury except for the red slash of the scar on his cheek. "False treachery! I mean to save the land from every penny in the kingdom going to England!"

"Never!" shouted the Earl of Angus. "We will never agree to an English rule!"

"Save it by selling it to England, you mean." Douglas

sprang onto the dais with the Earl of Angus following behind him. He strode two steps to stand face-to-face with the king. My cousin's mouth was a furious slash in his dark face. "We will stop you."

Douglas grabbed at David's surcoat. I lunged and shoved him back. His hand dropped to his dagger.

The bishop hammered his crook on the wooden floor of the dais, and it resounded like a drum. "Stop! Stop, I say!" He shoved the crook between Douglas and me. "Else you suffer the church's wrath!"

Douglas stopped, his mouth open, and stared at the bishop. I raised my hands and stepped back. Such fierceness from the bishop was like a slap in the face, but he may have saved us from open war. His glare swept across the room. The only sound was Douglas's heavy breathing.

"Now, remember you are in council." He banged his crook once more for emphasis. "Behave as is fitting!"

David nodded to de Landallis, paused, and then resumed his seat. Most of the men on their feet gradually followed suit, but Angus stood, fist clenched. Douglas still had not moved.

"Dunbar, I intend to honor you with more lands to make up the loss," the King said, his face stiff and voice hoarse.

Outraged muttering and cursing spread through the chamber.

"I willnae agree to it," Dunbar snarled. "Parliament willnae agree to it. I promise you that!"

The King looked at the men who had objected most vociferously. "If that plan cannae be agreed to, then we must make another plan to pay the ransom because there willnae be the funds in the treasury next year. You ken taxes havenae been coming into the exchequer."

Douglas stepped off the dais and threw himself down

beside Dunbar so hard that the bench creaked. "After the burning and destruction, I cannae collect more than I have been."

He was lying, but I decided this was not the time to say so. We had come close enough to blood flowing. I stepped back to stand behind the king, hand on the hilt of my dagger.

The bishop cleared his throat. "I will appeal to the pope to allow you to take ten percent of the church's tithe for two more years, Your Grace. To save the kingdom, he may agree when I make my case in the strongest possible terms. He doesnae want more war here."

"Thank you, Your Excellency. That would aid us greatly, but we cannae count on his agreeing or on his aiding us forever."

"I will gather an embassy to go to Avignon immediately. It is too urgent to wait."

David nodded to the bishop but turned to glower at one noble after another. "The revenue from the taxes must be improved if you willnae agree to my proposal." His hands were shaking, and he clasped them into fists as he rose. "This council is ended." He turned on his heel, his back to the muttering men who filed through the door of the screen that separated the hall from the main door.

"I will lead the embassy myself, Your Grace," the bishop said. "Especially when I relate these events, I believe I can convince him that you must have part of the tithe. He wants peace between England and Scotland. I fear that is what is at stake."

David rubbed the back of his neck. "I pray so, Your Reverence, because I havenae more arguments to convince Edward to give up my ransom."

Will furled his forehead. "But you must have kent they wouldnae accept an English king."

"Only an heir until I have a son."

James had wandered to the tall windows that faced into the bailey. "Sire, something is going on out there."

I started to go see what he was talking about, but stopped at a shout. "My lords!" A rather smarmy knight by the name of Malise Hull dashed through the doorway in the screen and came to a halt, panting. "The Stewart's and John Menteith's men are in the bailey. They seized the guards on the outer doors!"

There were shouts and stomping past the passage. I reached for my sword before remembering that I was not wearing one. A guard tossed me one that I caught by the hilt. Will and John Preston dashed to stand beside me between the door and the king.

Robert Stewart and John Menteith stormed in, swords now belted at their sides. Douglas, Mar, Dunbar, and Angus followed. Then their men-at-arms came in and took places around the room, pikes in hand.

My heart was thudding hard enough to beat its way out of my chest, yet I felt cold. Entering the king's presence bearing a sword was a crime. At least the swords were not in their hands, but I dared not turn to see if David was still there. Then I realized he must be when Stewart shouted, "I say that the council isnae yet ended!"

David's voice was surprisingly steady when he replied, "Very well, nephew. If you have aught to say, let me hear it."

"Thomas Murray has granted me the lands of Schenbothie in free barony that you havenae confirmed. To show your good intention, if you have such, confirm the grant. And swear that you relinquish the plan to make any Englishman your heir."

I turned slowly, careful not to startle a gang of armed and angry men, so I could see David. His hands twitched, but he hid them behind his back; his face was calm, but his eyes were not. They blazed with fury.

"I always intended to confirm the grant, Robert. But have you another plan to keep the peace if we cannae make the payments to England?"

Stewart's sword made a swishing sound as he drew it. "Aye. We name another king! Why should I wait to inherit to take the crown?"

"Sheath that sword!" the bishop bellowed, hammering his staff on the ground. "It is treason to draw it in the king's presence!"

Douglas laid a hand on Robert Stewart's arm, but glared at me. "Peace, Robert. I dinnae want a civil war. The King has been poorly advised by those with him. If he agrees to end the tax on our lands and accept our advice on all matters, I am willing to stay my hand."

I held my breath. If David did not agree to their demand, I had no doubt we were dead men.

The king's face was ashen, but the scar on his cheek had blushed scarlet. "Very well," he said in a choked voice. "I agree."

"At our next council, we might discuss raising money for the ransom," the Douglas said. "Though if King Edward wants a fight, that would suit me even better."

"There is more!" Mentieth shouted. "Restore my right to the lands of Knapdale. John Logie has nae right to them!"

The muscle in David's jaw twitched, but he nodded to Menteith. "I was advised by...a certain person who he had the right, but I see I was poorly advised. So I will make a grant to you of it."

Mentieth blinked and stuttered, surprised at the king's agreement. Not that David had a choice. "Aye..." He cleared his throat. "Your Grace. Thank you."

David swept an icy gaze over the armed men before him.

"Then—" He glared at Stewart. "if my nephew agrees, this council is now ended." He turned on his heel and strode regally from the hall. After the door was closed behind, he drew his dagger and plunged it deep into its planks. I would not lightly forgive this day, though payment might not be quick. For now, we were in a trap.

CHAPTER ELEVEN

March 1360, Edinburgh Castle

Will stood fidgeting outside the arched wooden doors of Saint Margaret's Chapel. Beside him, David and I waited, Cateline at my side, in our best finery. Bishop de Landallis was resplendent in gleaming white robes edged with gold.

A robin burst from a roof across the street, with a *twiddle-ooo — twiddle-eeede*, and then it disappeared from view.

Will smoothed the front of his tunic and his cloak. I chuckled at him and knocked into him with my shoulder. "Dinnae be so nervous you cannae do your job." I winked.

He started to answer, but stopped. Around the corner of the keep, onlookers were cheering for Isabella's procession. In the month since the attack by the earls, there had been no celebration in Edinburgh. But this was a small victory, at least. It put the lands and power of the Earldom of Fife into Will's hands and, therefore, into the king's. This felt like a beginning of the turn of the tide. But when David smiled, it did not reach his eyes.

The music of flutes, trumpets, lutes, and drums drifted in the air. Then they rounded the corner. Leading the way, James carried a large, silver goblet overflowing with roses, ivy, and red ribbons. The Earl of Mar led the palfrey, for none of Isabella's family were there to do the honors.

Isabella was a handsome widow nearing thirty, dressed all in green silk. Her bodice was right with a long, flowing skirt and a circlet of roses about her brow over a gossamer veil covering her hair as she was a widow, not a maiden. Musicians strolled after her palfrey, and then came a brightly dressed crowd, and their happy chatter blended with the music.

Will stared at his feet for a moment, and his throat worked. I had never known Will to look so nervous, yet the bride to look so calm. But then, it was his first wedding, not hers.

Mar reached to help Isabella from her palfrey and led her to the church door. Will surreptitiously wiped his palm before he took her hand in his, which made me chuckle. She looked straight ahead at the bishop, but quickly cast Will a sidelong glance.

After a moment, as the chatter died, the bishop said, "William Ramsay and Isabella de Stewart, do you come here freely, without coercion to give yourselves in marriage?"

Isabella said a husky, "Aye." Will quickly added his assent.

The bishop nodded with an approving look and had them repeat the vows.

I took the broad gold band set with a ruby from where I had tucked it into my belt and handed it to the bishop. He blessed it and gave it to Will.

"With this ring, I thee wed: This gold I thee give, with my body I thee worship, and with all my worldly goods I thee endow." He slipped the ring a little way onto each finger, saying, in turn, "In the name of the Father, the Son, and the Holy Spirit." With the last phrase, he slid it onto her ring finger.

Cheers and whistles nearly drowned out the bishop's closing blessing. People surged forward, and a fresh-faced acolyte held up an alms bowl. Will slipped his arm around Isabella's waist, and she scooped up a handful of silver pennies and tossed them to the edge of the crowd where servants looked on. Everyone cheered, and she tossed the coins until the bowl was empty.

The King called out, "Musicians, play something merry to guide us." The lutist struck a chord, and the other musicians followed with a gay, tinkling melody. Everyone clapped, and some joined hands for a circle dance.

"Lead the way to the feast." Smiling, David gave Will a push. There had been few smiles from him recently, so even that was good to see.

Will pulled Isabella's hand closer, keeping her at his side as the music pulled them around the keep to the door. I followed with the King, the bishop, and Mar. The rest of the crowd fell in behind, chattering, jesting about tonight's bedding ceremony, and laughing.

A guard in the King's livery opened the door for us, and they entered. The musicians climbed to the small gallery and struck up a tune. The shutters were thrown back, so that sunlight flooded in across the hall. Rushes sweetened with heather blossoms covered the floor and perfumed the air. Long trestle tables draped in white cloths were set with gleaming pewter goblets.

He guided her past the hundred or so guests as they stood in their places. They stepped onto the dais and stood to the right hand of the King. Cateline and I followed to the high table, and I carefully held her elbow as we went up the steps as she was heavy with our child. Sometimes the rush of joy and excitement was almost more than I could bear. None of us Douglases were fair to look at, so I hoped he would look like her. I tried to imagine it. But I then shook off the silly fantasy.

"Be seated, my friends," David said as he sat, Katherine

next to him. On the other side of the King, Domhnall of Lennox, Earl of Lennox, sat with his wife. Joanna de Moravia joined us at the high table, which was suitable for her station, though she looked forlorn. Beside Isabella, Douglas and his wife, Margaret of Mar, took their places, and beyond them, I took my place, closer to my cousin than I would have preferred. The bishop rose and gave the blessing.

Servants scurried to serve the wine. When everyone's cup was filled, the King stood and raised his wine cup. "To the bride and groom!" I leapt to my feet with the rest of the guests. We shouted and cheered and then drained our cups.

Once we were all seated again, Will motioned for her wine cup to be refilled. He whispered something to her. She covered her mouth with her hand, but her eyes were bright with laughter.

The trumpets blasted to announce servers carrying enormous platters of venison haunches with pepper sauce. Other platters were piled pheasants stuffed with apples and plum and currant tarts.

Will put the choicest bits of food on Isabella's trencher. She looked pleased.

More courses followed. Jaquet, Etienne, and Perrette entered. The two young men played their instruments as Perrette sang several songs. At the end of the course, they launched into *I Long for Thy Virginitie*, drawing cheers and pounding on the table from some of the more inebriated nobles. They withdrew with yet another purse of silver from the king.

Cateline whispered to me, "It seems very strange to me not to perform with them."

I added a bit of the venison on her trencher and nodded toward Will and Isabella. "They seem happy enough with each other." Of course, the marriage was not of their choice. One married to please one's lord. What Will had heard, that she was a pleasant person who would suit him, seemed true. And it seemed to suit her as well. I motioned for Cateline's cup to be filled with mead.

Watching Isabella, she said, "I think you are right."

"I cannae remember a time when he wasnae my best friend." I took a sip of the rich, fruity claret. "It doesnae always work out that way, so I am happy for him."

The first course was cleared and a subtlety representing spring with a young man and a tree made of marzipan. Another course came. Almond cream. Whole salmon cooked with apples. Cheese tarts. Shrimp and rice in saffron sauce.

Cateline nibbled at the food. "There is no room in there for more," Cateline said, eyes dancing. "That babe of yours must be very large."

A troop of tumblers ran in. She laughed as one juggled flaming torches while another had a dog dressed as a jester in a belled fool's cap that jumped through a hoop, and a third did cartwheels around the room. I squeezed her fingers, and she smiled at me from the corner of her eyes.

The feast had grown noisy. John and the Earl of Douglas guffawed at some jest they shared. Jugglers tossed the lit torches back and forth. James argued with another squire over the best dog for hunting wolves. Domhnall of Lennox loudly called for a dancing bear, complaining that the tumblers were boring.

"There was nae dancing bear to be found," I told him.

The King dismissed the tumblers and called for more music from the gallery. He drained his wine and returned to pressing food and drink on the guests. He drained his own as soon as it was refilled. Katherine whispered something to him and he smiled. Only she had lightened his mood these past months.

When the last course was down to a few broken tarts, the Countess of Mar leaned toward Isabella. "It's time, my dear."

She looked past Douglas to his wife, her daughter, and motioned for her to join them. She asked Joanna, "Will you aid us, Lady Bothwell?"

Joanna smiled her assent and turned to Katherine. "I ken it isnae custom, but will you nae aid us?"

Katherine beamed. It was not usual for an unmarried woman to take part, so she clapped her hands and hugged Joanna. "I will be honored."

Isabella stood. Cheers rang across the hall, and everyone raised their cup. Will patted her arm and would have spoken, but she shook her head. "I am fine, my lord." Her face was rosy with blushes, but she gave Will a little wave. The three women escorted her up the stairs toward one of the bedchambers.

Will drained his cup to the sound of cheers and taunts.

"What are you waiting for, Will?" I demanded.

"Give them a little time." He swirled the wine in his cup and tried his best to look unconcerned. James shouted that Will must be frightened by the bedchamber. One of the women yelled some very frank advice about what to do, to loud laughter.

The King stood, his face flushed from drink. "Now, up you go to do your duty." He grasped Will by the shoulder and turned him toward the stairs. Giving in to the inevitable, Will good-naturedly let us jostle and shove him up the stairs. The remaining women followed, several adding to the advice he had already been given.

Joanna met us at the door and indicated that Isabella waited in bed. I shoved Will through the door and unbuttoned his surcoat. My laughter bubbled up when he slapped my hands away. Sir John was untying his hose from his breech belt, intending to strip him. Herries helped me hold him when he tried to escape. The King said to hurry because it was rude to keep a lady waiting. All the while, Will batted, laughing, at our hands.

Alexander Haliburton folded down the coverlets on this side of the bed with a "Pardon me, my lady." Douglas was slinging pieces of Will's clothing onto a nearby chair, and the advice grew louder and more raucous. The women's particularly specific. Joanna looked on, blushing as she chuckled at the antics.

At last, with Will completely stripped and loudly expressing his objects, between bouts of laughter, a dozen of us lifted and flung him into the bed, where he bounced.

"Now, dinnae forget what I telt you," one of the women shouted, as we crowded, many stumbling from drink, out the door and closed it behind us.

"I dinnae need any advice, I thank you," Will bellowed.

Isabella was giggling as he slammed the door. Indeed, I thought they would do well together and my chest swelled with happiness for them.

CHAPTER TWELVE

April 1360, Edinburgh, Scotland

I rode around the corner of the two-story timber house with a recently re-thatched roof. The side passage led around to the back where the usual stable, kitchen shed, wash house, privy, well, and chicken coop were set in the icy yard. My stable boy took my reins when I swung from the saddle.

Pleasantly tired from a meeting with the constable, who was keen for my approval for improvements to the city walls. Finding the money had been a struggle with our straitened funds, but I had succeeded. It would quiet the constant complaints from the burgesses, not that I could blame them. We never knew when those walls might save lives.

I frowned toward the cook shed, where there was no sign of cooking, looking forward to a quiet November evening with a hot supper and some claret to savor. I opened the door and stepped inside to come to a halt as the woman we had hired as a midwife, Mistress Coults, bustled up the stairs to the bedroom, carrying a birthing stool. Our servant filled a pitcher with hot water heated over the hearth and hurried after her and closed the door. Jacquet stood, arms crossed, looking put out.

I snapped my mouth closed and hurried up the stairs, my heart speeding up. The midwife was setting down the stool. Cateline, lying in bed, turned her head and looked past the woman. She smiled at me and gave a little wave.

Mistress Coults whirled and flapped her apron at me. "Out! Being here doesnae befit a man!"

"But this morning—"

"I havenae time for talk, and this be woman's business." She flapped her apron some more. "It will be hours yet. Now go."

I backed out of the room. Mistress Coults had said that the bairn would come soon, but this morning Cateline had bustled about, moving the cradle and stacking bundling clothes with no sign that it would be today.

My chest swelled so much with pride that I could not contain it. "I am about to be a father!"

Jaquet crossed his arms. "I tried to see my sister. They threw me out as well, said it was no place for a man."

"How long...?" I waved a hand toward the upstairs.

"I am not certain. I came half an hour ago. I was going to send for you, but the midwife told me it would be hours yet." He grimaced. "She said you would only be underfoot."

Etienne barged through the door, panting. "I told the burgess that we could not perform this night. He was not pleased."

Jaquet gave an expressive shrug. "It cannot be helped. I am not leaving until my nephew is here." He paused, his mouth open as Perrette clattered down the stairs.

"Mistress Coults is sending me for more cloths." She rolled her eyes. "I think she just wants me out of her way."

An "Ow!" emanated from the bedchamber. It sent her scurrying on her errand. I wandered around the hall. Jacquet stared into the fire on the hearth. Etienne sat, chin in his hands. There were no more noises from the bedchamber except the occasional sound of footsteps.

When Perrette returned, arms piled up to her chin with linen cloths, I stopped her with a hand on her shoulder. Obviously, we were neither needed nor wanted here. "We are going to the White Hart. When there is news, come fetch me!"

She nodded and hurried up the stairs. I tilted my head to the door, and the others rose and followed me to the tavern. My stomach grumbled, but what I wanted was a large cup of wine. Probably several.

"Do you ken how long these things last?" I asked. I had never had any reason to pay attention to such things. He shook his head.

We sat around a table in the corner and the innkeeper brought us a flagon of wine and cups. Jacquet filled them and I took a gulp.

Etienne tilted his head. "Remember when Perrin's wife gave birth?" He turned to me. "A flautist we knew in Poitiers. Mama went to help with the birthing and it took half the night for the babe to come."

I raised my filled wine cup. "To it soon being over!"

"To a nephew!" the others shouted. We knocked our cups together and drained them to the last drop to the cheers of everyone in the tavern.

After sighing at the thought of it going on all night, I called for bread, butter, and cheese. We ate them as the watery November light faded into evening darkness. If the bairn had come, they would have sent me word. Of course they would. Everything was fine. Emptying the flagon of wine had settled my twitching nerves, but it had been so long. I needed to see for myself that there was no news.

I patted Jacquet on the shoulder and pointed my chin toward the door. The three of us returned to the house, and I rapped on the bedroom door.

Mistress Coults opened it a crack. "We will tell you when there is news." She closed the door in my face, but through it came the sound of a moan.

I scrunched my face and then relaxed it, trying to hold on to my patience.

Etienne shook his head and stirred up the fire. I sat in my chair before the hearth. The others pulled up a bench. Eventually, they stretched out on the floor before the hearth. We pulled our cloaks around us and made ourselves as comfortable as we could. I dozed, awakened when Perrette or our maid stumped down the stairs for water.

I jumped erect when Cateline screamed. The assistant bustled out of the house and returned with a basket filled with packets and jars of I knew not what. The sounds from within the bedchamber had grown worse, moans and cries of pain.

When the bells for Lauds tolled, I sat up, my head aching, for I had not slept for listening to the sounds of Cateline's travail. The evening and night had seemed weeks long. Women gave birth all the time. Most were fine. Most... "Should it take so long?" I asked.

Etienne shook his head. "I do not know." But his face was creased with worry.

The sounds from the bedchamber grew quieter, merely mewling, weak but frequent. My stomach tightened. I scrubbed my stubbly cheeks with a hand. "Etienne, fetch some ale from the tavern. My head is stuffed with wool."

He was back shortly and was filling our cups when there was a different wail—angry and indignant. I stumbled to my feet, pins and needles in my legs from sitting so long. They would call for me soon! As soon as the bairn was cleaned and swaddled! I swallowed the tightness in my throat and blinked. Those could not be tears.

Jacquet beamed at me. "Finally!"

The midwife's assistant burst through the door, kirtle raised as she ran through and out the door to the street. Jacquet's smile faded.

I went up the stairs and pushed the door open to stand on the threshold. The metallic stink of blood filled the air. Cateline was being half carried by Mistress Coults to the bed. Blood leaked down her legs. Perrette jostled a whimpering bundle in her arms. Gory cloths filled a large basket next to the red-smeared birthing stool.

The midwife lay Cateline down on the bed and lifted her legs onto it. She pulled up the coverlet and stroked her sweaty face with a damp cloth. There was so much blood. On the floor. On the midwife's arms. Spreading on the bed linens. Like the bloodiest of battlefields. I tried to speak, but words would not come.

"The babe..." Cateline whispered, her voice a mere thread, and her sister tucked the little bundle next to her head. Her face was the color of whey. Just yesterday morn when I rode out to the castle, her face was rosy. She laughed and sang and had blown me a kiss.

Mistress Coults turned to the door and motioned for me to come. My hand trembled when I brushed her cool cheek with my fingers.

"You will care for him?" Tears trembled in the corners of her eyes.

I knelt beside the bed and took her hand. They had not told me it was a son, but that did not matter. He was mine. "I swear it by Saint Bride. He is my son. Remember. I said we would name him William for my grandsire." I kissed her hand. She tried to squeeze my fingers, but it was only a feeble twitch. Her eyelids drooped, half closed.

When someone touched my shoulder, I looked up. Alexander Bur, Archdeacon of Moray, who was an old friend of the king's although a priest, said, "Word came it wasnae going well. The King thought I might be of aid."

He took my place, put holy oil on his fingers, and anointed her forehead and hands. "Through this holy anointing, may the Lord, in his love and mercy, help you with the grace of the Holy Spirit. May the Lord who frees you from sin save you and raise you up."

My throat closed up. I pressed my hand to my mouth to silence a wail.

Cateline, her travail over, seemed to sink into a soft sleep. I hoped so. No more suffering, dear one. The priest continued quietly saying the prayers for the dying.

Etienne dropped to his knees by the bed and crossed himself. The bairn made little sucking noises.

Cateline's breathing slowed, her chest barely moving. Then it moved no more.

The only sound was the rustle of the Bur's cassock as he rose.

I brushed a strand of hair back from her forehead. It was still damp with her sweat. She would hate that.

Then the bairn, still lying next to his mother, wailed, his red face screwed up in outrage. I slid my hands carefully beneath his body and lifted him. He was hardly bigger than my palms. I looked for a moment into his dark eyes. His tiny face was twisted into a fierce scowl. "Wilikyn," I whispered to him. Holding him close, I rubbed my cheek against the soft fuzz of his hair and closed my eyes to contain the whirlwind of loss and love.

"You will need a wet nurse," Mistress Clouts said in a prosaic tone.

"Then find one for me." I looked over the bairn's head as he nuzzled at my neck. "One you trust. He must lack for naught." Poor wee mite, he would lack for nothing except his mother.

"Aye. Now, let my daughter bundle him all tidy to be comforted." She turned to Perrette. "Lass, you make a milksop of the softest bread and warmed milk. That will do him well until I return. I ken just the woman for a wet nurse." She shook her head, looking down at Cateline, and crossed herself. "I will leave you to have her prepared."

Bur laid a hand on my arm. "I will send someone to aid with preparing the body." He looked at the fussing wee mite in my arms and made the sign of the cross on his forehead. "Thanks be to God. He looks like a hearty lad."

CHAPTER THIRTEEN

June 1360, Edinburgh Castle

Edinburgh Castle

June 1360

One of the serjeants brought me word that a large entourage of monks befitting an important churchman was approaching up the steep road to the castle from Edinburgh. I brushed the wrinkles in my surcoat from bending over the tax accounts, though I had taken nothing of them in except that there was not enough money. When I rubbed my cheek, I wondered how long it had been since I shaved. It had not seemed to matter any more than the food I pushed away at the table. But I could not greet guests to the castle looking so.

I shaved, nicking my cheek and cursing as I blotted the blood. When I looked at the red splotch, my stomach heaved. The towel with the scarlet splotch could have been the linen in the bed where Cateline had lain. I had sent the bed, the mattress and all the coverings soaked with her blood to be burnt. I spat out the sour bile out of my mouth, scrubbed my cheek hard to get rid of the blood, and dressed in fresh doublet and hose to meet the monks.

The white-clad Cistercians reminded me of a flock of gulls, most of them mounted on mules but the abbot on a fine brown palfrey. The blue banner with gold fleur-de-lis fluttered overhead.

I bent a knee as William de St. Andrews, Abbot of Melrose Abbey, dismounted. He gave me his blessing as the stable boys scurried to take the mounts. We entered the keep on the importance of his mission to consult with Bishop de Landallis, who would leave within the week for Avignon. The King would be eager to hear what had been said about the vital mission of finance to the pope, as would I, so I begged the abbot to refresh himself in our best guest chamber and join the King to bless and partake in a fine dinner in two hours.

After a page led him away, I sent a squire running to summon Cateline's brothers and sister to perform for our guests. They would be well rewarded. Another went to tell the seneschal we had an important guest, so the dinner should be the best that could be managed on such short notice. It would be foolish not to extend every courtesy to the head of such an influential abbey. The abbot was angry with the Earl of Douglas, and we needed to keep him on our side. King David had kept his head low while he did everything possible to gather knights and nobles to his side. The one thing the nobles who had attacked him could not do was grant titles.

If the abbot objected to dining with the king's leman at the high table, he was diplomatic enough not to say so. Joanna de Moravia sat next to Katherine. She was, if not Katherine's lady-in-waiting, then her constant companion. The Earl of Angus, sitting beside Will and Isabella, talked of preparing to leave for Edinburgh for a short time to go to his own lands. Between bites over the decorous tunes played by Jacquet, the abbot asked the King if he had taken action against the Earl of Douglas, who had forced the abbey to pay him a tax on their profitable wool trade.

David slapped his hand on the table so that his wine goblet wobbled. "The abbey is under the king's protection, as it always has been." At the moment, there was little he could do to put an end to Douglas's interference with the abbey's trade in wool, but the abbot chose not to mention it.

"Has the bishop left for Avignon?" I asked. As important was finding enough money to make the 10,000 pound yearly payment on the king's ransom while still having enough money to run the government. Without the land tax, that would be even more important, and I had spent days pouring over our taxes to find every penny that could be legally gained. It was not enough.

"They plan to leave in a week." He spoke at length about the canons who would travel with the bishop to help him convince the pope to grant King David a tenth of the church's tithe for three years. He then expounded upon the bishop's argument, the legalities that would be put forward, and the best way to increase taxes.

"What about Galloway?" I asked. "They are in open rebellion."

David grimaced. "They must be dealt with, but I think we delay that until the earls are no longer a threat."

Beside the king, Katherine Mortimer nodded with a surprising interest in what the abbot said. When he broke off to moisten his throat with some wine, she leaned forward. "Forgive me, Father Abbot, but did I hear true that Melrose Abbey has a relic of Saint Anne?"

"Indeed, Lady Katherine, we have that blessing." He turned an approving smile on her. "King David, first of that name and of blessed memory, acquired a finger of the mother of the Virgin Mary for us shortly after he had the abbey founded."

"Saint Anne is kent for her special care for women in childbearing. Or so my mother told me."

David beamed at her and laid his hand on hers.

"Are you traveling directly to Melrose, Father?"

"I am. I cannae be too long from my duties there, so we depart on the morrow."

She turned to the king. "Your Grace, I am sure the abbot would welcome the added safety of an armed escort." Her voice became uncertain, as though she was not sure what reaction to expect. "And I am going to go pray there for my safe delivery. To Saint Anne and the Blessed Mother, to whom the abbey is dedicated." She placed his hand on her stomach. "If I pray where there is such a relic, I am sure the saint will intercede for me."

David looked at her closely. "Are you sure that such a ride might not be a danger? You must take every care, my love."

"Women ride when much further along than I am." She gave me a kindly look. "So much can go wrong and..." Her voice wavered. "I want the good saint's protection."

A band tightened around my chest and I could hardly breathe. My hands were shaking, so I grasped my wine goblet tight and managed a courteous dip of my head to her.

The King said, "If my lady wills it, then so it shall be. We will escort the father abbot on the morrow, Archie. See to it."

The bell of Saint Margaret's Kirk rang for Prime. Outside, the white-clad Cistercians were mounting their mules. Joanna de Moravia was already mounted. A man-at-arms knelt and offered cupped hands as the King assisted Katherine into the saddle. He arranged her skirts for her. He kissed her hand and mounted.

I hurriedly swung into the saddle. The King and

Katherine led the way down the hill and through Edinburgh as the businesses were opening their shutters on the main thoroughfare. The passersby stood aside as we clattered past the little wind rustling the lion-rampant banner.

Despite the company of monks, it was a cheerful group enjoying the late summer sunshine. The hills were vast spreads of purple heather. In the fading gorse bushes, thrushes and warblers were noisily chattering. Overhead, a hen harrier drifted, too lazy in the warmth to bother to take any prey. When the golden coin of the sun reached its height, we would reach Newbattle Abbey, where we could stop to take dinner and let the mounts rest. The men-at-arms, riding on each side of the monks and knights, took up a ditty, one of the cleaner ones. I pulled up to be sure they were keeping in line but let them have their song, but I decided to send out extra scouts.

Malise Hull leaned toward John Preston, grinning as he spoke. Sir John threw back his head and guffawed.

Katherine slowed the pace of her palfrey until she rode beside the two men. "Laugher and singing need to be heard more here. Dinnae you think?" She looked around and pointed at a skylark, singing as it took flight. "See, it agrees."

I kneed my mount and rode ahead to catch up with the king. He glanced behind him and turned to me. "Och, Archie, seeing her happy is a joy."

I patted my horse's neck and forced a smile.

A shriek ripped the air.

John Preston shouted, "Hull! You Hellspawn!"

Hooves pounded. I hauled into a turn and kneed my horse to a canter. Preston knelt beside a shape on the ground.

"Katherine!" David sped past me.

Preston jumped to his feet and pointed toward the fleeing man. "He stabbed her!"

"James! Corbyn! With me!" I spurred my mount to a

gallop, leaning forward and shortening my reins. Shouts and cries of horror drifted behind me, but the drumbeat of hooves soon drowned them. Nothing mattered but riding Hull down.

He turned off the road to go cross country. I racked my brain to remember what the ground was like ahead. It was a patchwork of hills, but what ruts might be there to trip and break a horse's legs? I did not know. With this thought uncomfortably in mind, I urged my horse on as Hull disappeared over the nearest hill. It was deep with heather and heavy going, but I urged him to keep to a gallop. His neck was lathered and sweat flying, and he could not keep up this pace much longer. But then, neither could Hull's horse.

We topped the rise, and to my relief, the whoreson was only halfway down the slope. I risked turning my head. James and Corbyn were only a few horse lengths behind me, so they could continue the chase if I took a fall. I slowed to a canter, sweating almost as much as the horse.

Hull looked over his shoulder and began beating his mount with his reins. His mount showed no sign of flagging. He was pulling ahead, so I set my mount to a gallop again.

Ahead, a heather-covered hill rose sharply to its rounded summit. Young pines and gorse bushes flowed around its edges like the sea around a rock, too thick to be penetrated. Hull flung a look over his shoulder. A mistake.

The horse gathered his hindquarters beneath him and thrust himself over a fallen trunk. It stumbled upon landing. Hull flailed and nearly came off, clinging to his pommel with one hand and the horse's mane with the other. One leg was still across the high-backed saddle. The reins swayed near the horse's feet as it slowed and tossed its head at the unaccustomed position of its rider.

I bent forward, urging the last bit of speed from my mount, panting and sweat running down my face. I bent sideways and grabbed the reins. The horse snorted and came to a halt.

Hull turned loose and fell to the ground. He rolled to his feet. His mouth was open, eyes rolling as he looked for some escape. I drew my sword and dropped the point to his throat. My blood pounded in my ears, more from rage than exertion. But the bull's pizzle deserved no painless death. Besides, I suspected he was not alone in his crime. Who had put him up to foul murder?

Accompanied by men-at-arms, a cortege of monks with a bier bearing Katherine's body on lay brothers' shoulders was beginning its solemn way toward the nearby Newbattle Abbey. I realized Joanna must have accompanied them. David stood watching their dust, his gaze vacant, surrounded by Sir John and the rest of the knights.

I jerked Hull from his horse by his bound hands and threw him down at the king's feet.

David rubbed his chest, his surcoat splotched with gore. "She received Holy Unction before she...."

I made the sign of the cross.

The King looked down at the man face down before him. His gaze grew intense. "Who ordered it?" He kicked Hull in the side. "Who plotted with you?"

The murderer inhaled deeply, his nostrils flaring. He kept his eyes fixed on the ground. "No one. I kent she was behind your plotting."

I jerked him to his feet. Holding his arm, I backhanded him across the face. He stumbled backward, but my grip kept him on his feet. I hit him again. "The truth," I snarled.

He spat out a gobbet of blood. "It is."

"You wouldnae have acted alone." I pulled back my fist

and sunk it into his belly. He doubled over, and I let him sink to his knees. I was breathing fast. My heart thudded with fury. "You were trying to reach someone who would protect you." I kicked him flat on his back and it felt good.

The King crossed his arms. "A dose of the rack would loosen his lips. Mayhap, we should wait until we reach Edinburgh and use that." He looked toward the path the cortege had taken. "And I must see..." His voice broke. "I must see to my dear lassie."

Sir John shoved Hull over onto his side and kicked him. "They say the rack is the best for getting the truth from scurvy miscreants."

Curving my lips into a smile, I pulled him to his feet again. "I think more personal attention will break him. I can break his bones. One...at...a...time." I pulled his bound hands toward me, grasped his middle finger, and bent it back until it snapped.

He shrieked and jerked his hands to his belly, bending over them. He whimpered, and I felt my rage grow.

"Go, Your Grace. By the time you return, I shall ken the truth. No need for you to dirty your hands with this plague sore."

David slowly nodded and turned away. Sir John led his mount to him.

As he mounted, I grabbed Hull's hand and snapped another finger like a twig. "Let us see how you like this." I grabbed his thumb.

"No!" he screamed. "It was Angus. The Earl of Angus. He said if I did it for him—" He sobbed and dropped to his knees, cradling his hand against his belly. "He said he would give me enough that I would be a rich man after I fled to England."

David's face worked.

"Have him taken to Edinburgh. I havenae time for him

now." He bent his head, and tears ran down his cheeks for the first time. "I must go to the monastery to prepare for the funeral mass."

"He may still be at Edinburgh." I was tempted to kick Hull again, but instead, I called James and Preston to join me, grabbed a fresh horse, and we rode hard for Edinburgh. At Netherbow Gate, a guard gave us the news that the earl had left only a half hour before. Our horses were nearly done, so it took a few minutes to get fresh mounts and half a dozen men-at-arms to ride with us. Varying between a gallop and a canter to keep our horses from being blown, the sun was setting though the midsummer sky was still light when we caught up with him and his men.

They had stopped by a burn and dismounted to water their horses. Perhaps they meant to camp for the night. I did not ask. When I dismounted, there was a look of shock on his face. He smiled, but the look of suspicion in his eyes gave him away.

Hate is a strange thing... I had rarely felt it. I fought from duty and not from hatred. But when I looked at him, all the emotion in me and my grief turned to hate. I thought of Katherine, whose child would never draw breath. I thought of my own bairn who would never know a mother and my heart ache turned to cold hate. I wanted to cut him down and feel his blood thick and warm on my hands as he died.

James took a step forward, but I said, "Leave him to me. Kill his men if they interfere."

I stepped forward and raised my sword high over my head.

Preston shouted, "Dinnae kill him!" I stopped listening. My only thought was watching Angus's eyes to gauge his next move.

He came at me. One moment his sword was pointed toward my feet. The next, he stepped forward and slashed up.

I stepped back. When he brought his blade down, I stepped back in. I caught his sword in a bind. Still pushing, I slid to the side, shoving my leg behind his. Then I used my greater height to shove him backward over my leg and flat on the ground.

I raised my sword, but he was already rolling. He hooked my foot with his and jerked it out from under me. I staggered and flailed to keep my balance. The bull's pizzle kept rolling and came to his feet, his sword pointing at my face. He slashed. I caught his sword on mine, and he thrust toward my chest. I twisted to the side. His momentum kept him coming, and my sword tip cut his cheek open. Blood dripped down his face and off his chin. I smiled, knowing I had him.

Grimacing with desperation, he rushed me and hacked a side slash. I stepped to the side, pommeled my sword, and slammed the hilt into the back of his head. The blow dropped him face down. He was still breathing, so I raised my sword.

I was yanked backward, and I slammed backward with my elbow. It drew a pained grunt.

"Stop!" James shouted. "He is done. Now, he is the king's!"

I lowered my sword, my chest heaving as I glared at the murderer, lying face down on the ground. "He deserves to die," I growled.

"He does," Preston said, "but that is for the King to decide how. Not you."

I gripped my sword as the desires warred inside me. I wanted his blood, but a lifetime of serving my King was even stronger. Finally, I nodded. Thomas of Angus would die. Just not today.

CHAPTER FOURTEEN

January 1361, Linlithgow Palace

There was a burst of gray wings against the clear winter sky, and a pigeon veered off with a whirring trill. The hundred or so members of the king's entourage who had arrived with him from Edinburgh stood waiting for the ceremony. Workers who had stopped the work on Linlithgow's walls, ordered to honor the king's coming, stood around the edges of the crowd. The ground and buildings were covered with a gossamer veil of stone dust from repairs. Gusts of the winter wind raised it in eddies.

The King and I stood before the arched wood doors of the Church of Saint Michael.

He put his hand on my shoulder and turned his back to the crowd. "Archie, I have just made a decision."

I raised my eyebrows in question. "About executing Angus?" The earl was deep in a dungeon in Dumbarton Castle, a harsh fate, but I still thought he should be hanged, drawn and quartered.

David pressed his lips into a hard line. "Dying is too easy for him." His icy voice was sharp as an executioner's axe. "He will rot there and the rats shall eat his corpse."

"I wanted to see his traitor's blood, but the picture of rats chewing off his face while he still lives is a good one, Sire." He was not one to pronounce he had made decisions without cause, so I was curious. "So what decision is it?"

"The estates that just came to Joanna de Moravia since her husband died must be protected. Robert Stewart thinks he can grab a third of them through his son's marriage to Bothwell's widow."

I nodded, trying to look like I was following his point, but I did not know what that had to do with me.

"Forbye, she is the daughter of a dear comrade-in-arms. I would see her and her baronies protected. The lady must be married as soon as possible to someone who can do that. I mean that to be you."

It felt like he had punched me and I must have gone white from the look on his face. I opened my mouth and closed it, speechless.

"Marriage has little to do with love, Archie. You ken that. I need a man strong enough to hold her lands and fight off the Stewarts if need be. There is no one else I can count on to do that. And if I dinnae see her married, there is the risk someone will take her by force. I willnae take that risk."

Her father had been one of the king's closest advisers. She was the granddaughter and great-granddaughter of multiple earls. From her father and from her husband, she had a claim to lands that scattered from the castle-barony of Bothwell to the barony lands of Stonehouse in Lanarkshire and others almost too numerous to count.

I knew he was right. Marriage was a matter of power, land and title. He knew that better than most since they had married him to Joan when he was five years old. Stifling a sigh, I asked, "Have you told this to the lady?"

"Nae. But I will after this other business with James is done."

I crossed my arms, looking at my feet as I thought it over. I had no objection to the lady. She was attractive, and we were friendly enough, though nothing more. I could have never married either of the women I had loved. He would never have agreed. A connection to the Douglases was too valuable to waste. Then I remembered something that he might have forgotten or not known. "The lady and I are cousins, though." I frowned, trying to remember exactly how. "In either the third or fourth degree. I dinnae recall which. So, we would need a papal dispensation."

"Easily enough done." He tapped his fingers on his leg. "The request must be sent immediately. I want as little delay as possible." He nodded briskly. "Now, let us have this done. I am sure James has had enough praying."

He summoned James, who knelt before him on the hard-packed dirt. The King tapped with a sword first on one shoulder and then on the other. He held out his hands, and the newly made knight made his oath of fealty. As the King buckled a sword belt around James's waist, I knelt and fastened on his gold spurs. The crowd cheered.

The King clapped him on the shoulder and motioned the Stewart and the Douglas to join us. "A charter granting you lands in Dumphrieshire awaits us." His mouth twitched.

"Your Grace!" James colored with excitement. "I didnae expect any lands so soon."

I stifled a grin. That would be among other grants of land hemming in Douglas and Stewart. I was tempted to go with them to the signing just to see the looks on their faces, but it had nothing to do with me.

Margaret Drummond swayed her way to David's side. "I love seeing a knight dubbed. Such a braw sight, and you lend it great dignity, Your Grace." She turned her honeyed smile onto James. "And you as well, Sir James."

James bowed to her. "Thank you, my lady."

The King smiled. "Then I must dub more knights, since it pleases you so."

I bit the inside of my cheek to keep from sneering. Since her husband died, she had constantly found reason to be near the king. At first, deep in grief, he had seemed hardly to notice when she began to insinuate her way with him, but I found her as obvious as a town strumpet. The Drummonds were in a feud with the Stewarts over land. An alliance with her would only bring the threats of a civil war to a head. The King giving lands and titles that the earls wanted was a necessary provocation. Taking her as a leman was not. I made obeisance to the king, excusing myself.

The crowd had broken up into clumps sharing gossip or deciding whether hunting would be worthwhile as they began wandering into the donjon. Joanna of Moravia was chatting with Will Ramsay and his lady wife. I had not yet had a chance to give her my sympathies on the death of her husband in London, where he had been a hostage to guarantee the payment of the king's ransom. I hesitated, thinking of what I now knew, but they had seen me, so I strolled over.

Will slapped my shoulder. "Archie! How is that bairn of yours doing?"

"Given a chance, he tries to eat anything he can crawl to." A fond grin that I could not contain stretched my cheeks. "The wet nurse says it is my imagination that he calls me Da, but I ken she is wrong. And every time I see him, he has grown." I felt a bit foolish babbling on about a bairn, so I turned to Joanna. "I was sorry to hear the news about your husband. *Requiescat in pace*." I crossed myself.

"It was a shock. He was still a young man, but the plague..." She stared down at her clasped hands. "It is an awful way to die. We had little time together, which also makes me sad. I didnae even ken him well."

I was at a loss for what to say, so there was a pause. Fortunately, the countess put a hand on Joanna's arm. "That is hard, but I ken he was fond of you."

There was a brief pause. No one wanted to talk about the plague that was once again sweeping across England. Even the thought of it made me shudder. Better to die in battle than the horror of the buboes swelling until they burst as your life was sucked out of you.

"Why are we standing out in the chill?" Will asked, looking uncomfortable. He always did better with jests than solemnity. "There will be warm hippocras in the keep, or I will know the reason why."

I chuckled, and we joined the stream of nobles going inside. The screen wall a few feet into the hall closed off the opening. Beyond, the dais at the end was empty, but there was a roaring fire on the large hearth and servants with goblets of warmed hippocras and mulled wine and platters of cheese and onion tartlets. I took two cups of the wine, steaming and giving a scent of cinnamon, and handed one to Joanna. An uneasy feeling in my chest made me feel I was being dishonest. I pointed my chin toward the screen entrance. "Might I have a privy word, my lady?"

David might be irate at my having a word with her before he did, but if we were to deal together for the rest of our lives, I would start it with honesty. Everyone had entered, so it would be almost a private space, yet not so private as it would cause gossip. She looked up at me, puzzled.

"It shouldnae be for me to tell you, but I am nae a man fond of secrets."

Her thinly plucked eyebrows rose.

"The King isnae happy that you and your lands are without a lord's protection." This was even more uncomfortable than I had expected. After clearing my throat, I went on. "He means to send to the pope for dispensation for us to marry."

Her hand went to her mouth and her eyes widened.

As I hadnae been thrilled, I could hardly expect her to be. "If you hate the idea, I am sure we could talk him out of it. But he is determined that you must have someone able to protect you and your lands."

She snorted. "Mainly my lands."

"Aye, lands always matter. But truly, he respected and valued your father, so you matter as well. For your own protection from being taken by force, you need a husband." This was truly awkward. Perhaps I should have left it to the king, but it was too late to think of that. "If there is someone you prefer, tell me so and I shall argue for him with the king."

"And you, Sir Archibald? What do you prefer?"

"I hadnae thought of marriage, to speak true." I shrugged. "But I think we would well suit."

"As would the lands and baronies." She twitched a wry smile.

I propped a shoulder against the wall and took her hand. "As would the lands and baronies. The King intends to see that your father's and your husband's all go to you. And to your husband,"— My smile was as wry as hers— "which I wouldnae mind. They will need someone with a strong sword arm because the Stewarts willnae take it well. They have an eye on part of your husband's lands. A strong sword arm I can provide. It could well lead to a feud."

She paused. "Aye, that doesnae surprise me. Robert Stewart is a greedy man. As are his sons."

"But all the lands and titles in Scotland wouldnae make a good marriage if you hated it." I stroked the back of the soft skin of her hand with my thumb. "I would do my best to be a good husband. Nor am I one to raise my hand to a woman."

"You have a lad."

"William." There must be no doubt of this. "I recognized

him as my son and I will rear him. I will provide for him, though he willnae be my heir."

She tilted her head, looking me in the eye, and took a deep breath as though steeling herself. "Do you have a leman then?"

It had been hard getting through my grief, when even seeing someone happy had hurt. It had been my son who had pulled me through. "I—" I paused for a moment to control the stab of pain. "You must have heard that his mother died." It had been common gossip. "I havenae taken another, nor am I wanting one." I squeezed her hand slightly and straightened from the wall. "If ever I did, I wouldnae humiliate you by having her in your home or your sight. That is the best I can say, but I swear by Saint Bride on that much."

"And you didnae break your oath."

"Never." For some reason, her intense scrutiny made me smile. "So what will you tell the king? Whatever it is, I will agree to it."

She took back her hand, still studying my face. She nodded. "I shall consent."

She proceeded into the main room of the great hall and I followed. The King along with James and the two earls entered through a door that opened onto the dais. James was beaming, but the earls looked grim. Then it came to me what I should do, so I placed Joanna's hand on mine and led her onto the dais. Everyone had turned to look at us.

I bowed to the King and Joanna then turned to face the onlookers. I shouted, "I challenge any five men in the kingdom to joust against me for the hand of the Lady of Bothwell. If none can defeat me, I claim her hand in marriage as mine."

Joanna put her hand to her breast and her cheeks flushed bright pink. When I looked over my shoulder, David raised his eyebrows and looked like he wanted to laugh, but Robert Stewart's face was twisted in a fierce scowl.

The room was filled with noisy speculation and exclamations of surprise. Will shouted over the chatter, "A braw challenge, Archie! I am eager to see who dares to ride against you."

On the far side of the hall, a youth barely old enough for his spurs yelled, "I dare. I accept the challenge." He was unknown to me, but I had seen him in Stewart's following. No surprise there.

CHAPTER FIFTEEN

April 1361, Edinburgh, Scotland

The day of the challenge dawned with a smirr of rain, but by the time the bells rang for Terce it had stopped, though wispy clouds still scudded across the sky. "Not enough to make the ground too muddy. I hate riding the list in the mud," I told Gil as we rode our rounceys out of the gates of Edinburgh Castle. Gil and Colbyn were beside me and a dozen of my usual followers behind. One led my favorite courser and a spare mount in case he was injured.

Half of the city was out and about as the sun, half hidden behind scudding clouds, neared its height.

We made our way through the crowded streets, but business was slower than usual. Apparently, many businesses had given their workers time to go to the tourney, which allowed the maisters to go as well. The merket cross was clear of peddlers and beggars who must have decided they would do better where there would be a crowd. There was usually traffic coming into the city with wains piled with vegetables, peat, or chickens and ducks or people coming to shop, but today most of the traffic was going outward. People flowed through the crowded streets toward the massive Netherbow

Gate as the tourney was being held at King's Park. There were even strangers who had arrived yesterday and stayed in the city overnight from as far afield as Perth to see the outcome of the challenge. It was said that some of my opponents were armed and mounted at the cost of Robert Stewart.

A wain filled with ale barrels trundled out ahead of us. It would not surprise me if one of the taverns would sell mugs to the onlookers. Peddlers pushed carts filled with fresh bread and trinkets to hawk to the onlookers. I had ordered the constable and his deputy to have plenty of men to keep the peace. I also wanted them to listen for talk of the plague. There had been deaths in northern England. For weeks we had been sending up fervent prayers that it did not reach us this time.

Colbyn, riding beside me, muttered, "That pride will kill you, eventually. Riding five jousts in one day." He had been saying the same thing ever since I made the challenge.

I made my usual reply. "Have you ever kent me to lose?"

He leaned over to spit on the ground. "Have you ever ridden in five bouts in a row?"

I shrugged. "It is four passes each." A limit to the number of passes was usual. "I have fought longer in battles." He was convinced I suffered from hubris, too convinced I could not lose, not that he would call it that. Perhaps. But I had never been unseated in the list. I did not intend that today would be the first time. Even so, the day before, I had sent Colbyn, who was less likely to be recognized, to the tilting ground where the other contestants were practicing. He brought back a report that they had ridden well at the quintain, a post set up as a practice target with a sandbag attached that would swing around and strike an unsuccessful tilter. Many had ridden practice charges at each other along each side of the tilt. A couple even sword play for a time, which made me smile if they planned on unhorsing me.

"That Mathou de Blinsele is the one you want to watch," Colbyn said. "I would bet he be the one Strathearn is backing. Built like a bull, nearly as tall as you and even bigger through the shoulders. The rest be naught but unable worms! You will squash them underfoot."

I had no intention of ignoring his advice and afterward, I sent a couple of men to tamp down the earth that had been torn by galloping hooves. If the ground was too torn up, as was likely, they could do the same between bouts.

Outside the gate was a sprawl of small wattle-and-dob houses where the confined city spilled past its boundaries. The road marched straight ahead in the distance to the blue expanse of the Firth of Forth. To the right, beyond its stone fences spread the fields, gardens and expansive buildings of Holyrood Abbey. To the left, bound by a long withy fence, were the pastures and woods of King's Park beyond which hulked the gray prominence of Arthur's Seat.

Another hundred yards brought me to the gap in the fence. I led the way through and made for the far side where the tourney field was marked off with posts and ropes. Colorful pennants on tall poles flapped in the breeze around the list's arena. Yesterday, builders had erected fencing and stands for the tourney ground. A tent stood at each end where we contestants could withdraw to prepare. Opposite the halfway mark of the tilting fence were spectator stands with five levels of wide planks nailed to stout posts. The center beneath an awning was reserved for the King who had yet to arrive. A few noble spectators, both men and women in colorful clothes, had already taken their places. Along the rope boundaries, the spectators were gathering. The gamblers amongst them were loudly soliciting bets, competing to shout the best odds.

I made my way to the recet, the round tent I would use for preparation for each bout. Will was standing with James, lacking his usual grin. At the opposite end of the tourney field, another tent stood, crowded with my opponents, their squires, supporters, and mounts. I flung myself off my horse and clapped Will on the arm.

"Put down your wagers?" I asked.

He laughed. "Of course." He turned to walk away, calling over his shoulder. "The King wagered on you as well, so I suggest you win."

As I watched Will stroll to the stands, James said, "I laid the bets you wanted and some of my own."

"Well, I hope you found good odds." I chuckled. "And with someone who willnae have to be chased down to get our money."

"I had to find two to handle both our wagers. But we should make a good profit." He snorted. "You should let me have that. Some of those fools riding against you have braw enough harness and mounts you wouldnae miss it."

A man-at-arms with two pack horses had brought my armor and weapons earlier in the morning. Inside the tent contained only a small cot and a couple of stools. As Gil laid out my harness, the clamor of the crowd grew louder. Everyone in Edinburgh, and probably as far as Perth, had heard of the challenge.

"Sounds like you will have a good audience. They came to see you win," Gil said as he buttoned my quilted arming doublet.

"Most dinnae care as long as there is a good show."

Fastening the breastplate of my jousting cuirass to the back was a fussy job involving clasps down the sides, but Gil was fast at it after all his practice. He grumbled under his breath as he knelt to buckle the greaves around my legs. When I held out my arms to the side for him to fasten the rerebraces onto my upper arms, he muttered, "All this is going to be heavy after a few bouts."

"I have worn it through worse."

Gil smoothed the peacock feathers that served as a crest of my bascinet and put it over my head. He adjusted the straps and drawstring, so it was firmly in place and tugged the chain mail aventail to be sure my neck was protected. "No visor, aye?"

I nodded and sat on a stool so he could push the articulated sabaton on my feet with gold spurs already attached. I shoved my hands into my gauntlets and then Gil motioned for me to stand. He paced around me to examine his handiwork and then nodded. He held up the surcoat I had made for this tourney and slipped it over my head. It fell to my knees, the Douglas stars above the symbol for the heart of King Robert embroidered on the chest. Then he buckled on my swordbelt. Instead of my usual claymore, a smaller, dulled arming sword hung from it. Even though its edge was not sharpened, the point could kill, but today it would not.

James stuck his head in. "The King just took his place."

There was nothing more to be done, and I went out of the tent. James stood anxiously next to my gray courser that pawed and shook his head. I think he knew that when he wore the metal barding that protected his face and neck and flanks that there would be battle. The exclamations, shouts, and laughter blended into a loud drone. I grasped the cantle, stuck my foot in the stirrup, and threw myself into the saddle. Gil handed up my lance with its blunt tip spread out like a cup. He then held up my shield while I bent and slid my arm through the leather straps.

"Make sure there is plenty of water. And ale." I would need it. Already, even though the clouds cut off some of the sun, sweat was already beaded on my forehead beneath my helm. My biggest enemy would be the heat and exhaustion, not my opponents. "And tell them I am ready."

Gil trotted around to the front of the tent. A moment

later, a trumpet gave a sharp blast. A squeeze of my calves had my courser trotting past the tent and onto the field to earsplitting cheers, shouts, and a few jeers from the spectators.

The stands were crowded with upper-class spectators, mostly nobles but also some of the wealthier burghers and guildmaisters. At the top of the stands, King David sat beneath the awning. Margaret Drummond on one side was whispering to him. On the other, Joanna had her gaze fixed on me. Will was there, still looking unhappy. The Earls of Douglas and Strathearn sat together glaring, surrounded by their followers. Near them with his nephew and heir was the wizened Earl of Dunbar.

The crowd at the fences all the way around the field had grown to be three and four people deep. The shouts of hawkers and beggars added to the cacophony. Some enterprising traders had even set up trestle tables behind the crush. Scattered among them were enough of my constable's men to ensure that there would be no trouble.

Domhnall of Lennox had agreed to be a judge along with Thomas of Mar. They strode to the center of the field to await us. Domhnall was no friend to me, which suited Robert Stewart, but I was sure he had too much pride to allow anyone to be seen to break the rules, which would reflect on his honor. Thomas was such a renowned fighter, no one questioned his qualifications to judge.

The first rider was one of the 'useless worms' as Colbyn had called them. I suspected they were saving the serious opponents for when they thought I would be too tired to give a good fight. He rode toward Domhnall, his courser jittering and crow hopping as he cursed and tried to bring him under control. His squire stayed well out of reach of the hooves. Gil, as my squire, trotted behind me as I rode up to the midpoint of the field, my lance upright, and bowed to Lennox and Mar.

I could not help the flick of a smile when I confirmed my name to him as the judge and waited until the other man confirmed his. I would dispose of him too quickly for his name to matter to me. He glared at me briefly and called our names out to the herald, who checked them on his parchment and bellowed them out for the crowd.

Lennox waved us away, so I wheeled and rode to the far end of the field, lowered my lance, and hooked it into the arret so it would not slam backward on a hit. My gray snorted and pawed the ground. He raised his hand, and the trumpet blared again. I pulled my shield close and squeezed hard with my thighs and feet. My gray gathered his haunches and plunged to a gallop. We pounded alongside the flimsy barrier. I kept my shield straight to make the hit as hard as possible, but tilted my lance to his on the edge. His lance hit. It shattered, rocking me back. I was past him, my lance still whole.

I looked to the side and reined into a wide turn. He was perhaps better than useless, but no more than competent. The next pass would finish him.

By the time I galloped toward him, he had another lance and was spurring his horse to get it to a gallop. I hit him square in the middle of his shield and tipped him backward over his high cantle. He managed to grab hold as I passed, breaking his fall. I slowed, circled again, and cantered to await whether he would yield or fight on foot. He knelt in surrender.

The crowd shouted and cheered. I suspected few had wagered on whatever his name was. Back at the recet, I tossed down my lance. I had felt it crack on the second hit. I gulped down the ale Gil handed and took the fresh lance. It would be a long day.

CHAPTER SIXTEEN

As Colbyn had expected, none of the first four contestants were any strain, but I was drenched in sweat, and my mount was lathered. Knowing the last might be a challenge, instead of riding back to the recet, I rode to where Lennox stood at the midway of the field. "I need to change my mount, and the field should be smoothed. No point in one of our mounts breaking a leg."

He bellowed for some workers to tamp the hacked turf back into shape.

Even without being knocked from the saddle, the hammering of driving a lance into a shield at a gallop had me beginning to ache. I suppressed a groan as I climbed from the saddle.

Colbyn trotted up with my spare mount. Gil unfastened my helm and said, "There is a bucket of water inside."

I thrust my head all the way into the bucket, water slopping onto my feet. When I straightened, I shook my head hard, splattering it across the tent. "Time to finish this," I muttered. The one Colbyn had warned me of, Mathou de Blinsele, would be next.

Gil thrust another mug of ale into my hand. "It will take them a few minutes to knock the ground back into shape."

He was right, so I downed it, knowing I might need the energy for the coming bout. Colbyn pulled back the flap of the tent, letting me know the field was ready, so I tramped out and swung back into the saddle.

The trumpet brayed, and I trotted out from the recet, my fresh mount tossing its head in excitement. Both my coursers seemed to enjoy the attention and shouts of the crowd. The herald yelled out our names and de Blinsele went down to the far end, his fine courser prancing and his polished armor gleaming in the sun. Like me, he wore no visor the better to see and breathe. Colbyn was right. He was as almost as big a man as I, and the earl would not have provisioned him with such fine armor if they did not think he was good enough to win.

At a second blast, we thundered toward each other. I angled my shield to deflect the worst of the power as we slammed together. Even so, my back whacked against my saddle's high, hard cantle. We were past each other, both still upright in seconds.

I made a wide turn again to keep my speed up, but he did the same. We slammed into each other again. My lance shattered spraying splinters. Gil sprinted toward me, holding up a fresh lance. I grabbed it as I rode, and de Blinsele was almost on me. Trying to bring it into line, it barely scraped his shield. The blow of his lance lifted me out of the saddle, but I clamped my legs. It was pure strength in my thighs that kept me erect. We wheeled around for a fourth pass, lowered our lances, and charged. Once more, de Blinsele angled his shield to deflect the force, but I aimed and hit just the right spot. The impact lifted him up and sideways.

The onlookers were roaring with excitement.

He let the lance go so he could grab the pommel and held

on long enough to break his fall onto his knees, still holding onto his shield. He was back on his feet by the time I circled my mount and drew his sword. I slowed my mount to a walk and dropped my lance on the ground.

Gil ran out to take my reins as I dismounted. Fighting with arming sword and shield was never my preference, but it would do. My breathing slowed as calm washed over me. I bowed to de Blinsele and my blade slipped from the sheath with a whisper. It is difficult to hurt a man in plate armor with a sword, but the thin, articulated plate on the knee and the wrist are vulnerable. He was a big man, but it was easy to depend too much on size and strength. The Knight of Liddesdale had taught me better. Now I would see if anyone had taught him.

Warily, he advanced on me, shield raised. We circled, and I waited for an opening. With a shout, he slashed at my head. I caught it on the edge of my shield and backhanded a blow onto his shield that rocked him sideways. I was past him in an instant, turned, and smashed a blow to the back of his knee. He cursed.

The yells and shouts of the crowd were like the wash of waves on a distant shore. Lennox circled us, hovering just out of reach of a stray blow. Sir Walter Haliburton stood farther back.

He backpedaled. I lowered the point of my sword away from my right hip, inviting his attack. Let him think I was tiring after the many bouts. I hoped he would take the bait.

De Blinsele threw himself at me, bellowing as he hammered an overhand blow at my unshielded right shoulder. I sidestepped and cut upward. It caught his blade in a bind. Turning my wrist, I snaked my blade around his. He bulled forward. I smacked my blade on the back of his wrist as he passed.

I waited as he spun to face me once more. He turned his

wrist as though I had numbed it. Within the opening of his helm, his face was flushed, his eyes narrowed with anger. Several expressions flitted across his face as he decided on his next attack. Cautiously, he stepped forward, easing into range for another attack. His shield was angled to the side, and he raised his sword high, the point behind his head.

Without moving, I kept my shield high to protect my head and pointed my sword at his eyes. He feinted. I stepped back. I watched his eyes as I held my stance. He stepped forward again. I leapt toward him with a straight thrust at his chest. He caught it on his shield and pushed it to the side as he swung his sword in a horizontal cut. I caught it on my shield. We were almost chest to chest, and I let him push my sword as I stepped to the right. I shoved forward and slammed my sword down on his wrist again.

His sword flew out of his hand. Without meaning to, I burst out with a laugh.

Lennox threw up his hands to indicate a winner. The trumpet blared in response and the crowd went wild with shouts, cheers and some curses.

Instead of dropping to a knee in submission, de Blinsele turned and stepped toward his sword that was almost at Lennox's feet. The earl scowled at him and put his foot down on it. With a howl of rage, de Blinsele pulled the dagger on his right hip and drew back his arm. Still chuckling, I threw my arms wide. A dagger was not made for throwing and certainly would not pierce my cuirass. It hit my chest with a clank and fell to the ground.

A roar of outrage arose from the onlookers along the barrier ropes. Boos and hisses filled the air. The King had jumped to his feet, face twisted into a snarl.

Lennox ran at de Blinsele and shoved him with both hands, his face contorted with anger. "A pox on you! What do you think you are doing?" he shouted.

Haliburton stormed up and glared at the man. "You knave! You ken the rules of the tourney!"

"There isnae rule that I cannae keep fighting!"

"Have you gone mad?" Lennox thrust his face into de Blinsele's. "Was that dagger dulled?"

"Nae harm done. Just a bit of knightly temper," I called out. De Blinsele had not only used what I suspected was a sharpened weapon, the tourney had limited each bout to four passes and the sword fight counted as a fourth pass. But I had won and my opponent had only humiliated himself.

"You shame your knighthood! And your maister." Lennox stepped back and yelled for the herald to announce the winner. The trumpet blared again, and the herald bellowed that Archibald Douglas was the winner.

Haliburton snarled, "Now, send your squire to forfeit your armor and your horse." He stomped away.

Gil led my mount up, beaming. "I had better go collect our winnings!"

"Och, so you had." I took the reins and mounted. "I have a wedding to pay for."

CHAPTER SEVENTEEN

July 1361, Edinburgh Castle

I was once again with the constable, Simon Reed, going over the taxes, a task I grew to hate more every day. There was at least money in the treasury since the pope had agreed to give the King a portion of all tithes raised in the kingdom. With civil war still simmering, David decided to withhold this year's payment of his ransom. The English King grumbled, but I suspected he still believed one of his sons might be made David's heir. Though there was money in the treasury, it was being spent quickly. David still had not started the work on his long-planned new tower for Edinburgh Castle, but new stables had been built and large numbers of horses had been commanded to be purchased and there were the constant repairs to the walls. At the moment, the earls held their hands from another direct threat, and while they did, we prepared.

Reed was muttering that we should talk to the Burgess Hogg to see if he could suggest another means of raising taxes when there was a rap on the door. When I replied "Enter" one of the squires opened the door and said the King required my immediate presence and that of the constable.

Inside, two serjeants, armored and holding a glaive, stood guard next to the King on the dais. Bishop de Landallis stood next to him. I was surprised to see Will and most of the king's court in attendance. Reginald Keith, Marischal of Scotland, Robert Erskine, Malcolm Drummond, Niall Cockburn, Walter Murray, and John Maitland were there. Walter Haliburton must have just arrived, as I had not seen him before. The castle seneschal entered from a back entry at the same time as Sir John and I. But Dunbar, Douglas and Stewart were nowhere to be seen.

"My lords," said Will, his face ashen, "Word arrived yesterday at Dalhousie that Galashiels has been struck with the plague. A traveling trader brought it. He died the next day." He made a fist and slammed it on the long table. "Within a week, there had been—" He paced angrily back and forth across the dais. "—there had already been dozens of deaths. And the knight who carried word fell ill with it within hours after he rode in. I ordered the gates closed and rode to bring the news."

Icy fingers gripped the back of my neck and I shivered. I closed my eyes to block out the sight of friends, the black buboes bursting to pour forth foul puss, moaning in agony. "Once it arrives, there isnae way to halt it." I crossed myself.

I turned when someone cleared his throat.

John Hogg bowed. "You summoned me, Your Grace."

"Aye." The King motioned the wealthy burgess to come nearer. "The burgesses need to ken this news and take part in any decisions. You must represent them." He nodded to Will to continue.

"When I left Dalhousie before dawn this morning, only the one man was stricken, but as Sir Archibald said, once the great plague arrives, there isnae way to halt it. So it is only an hour from us now."

"Where is your lady wife?" I asked.

"Thanks be to God, she is in Fife and safe for now."

"Should we prepare to move the court, Your Grace?" the seneschal asked.

The hall broke out in a chorus of opinions at the wisdom or foolishness of such a move. A number pointed out that few nobles had died in the last outbreak. Will shouted that several knights had already died in Galashiels, and one was dying as we spoke back in Dalhousie. Someone protested that it might only be in Galashiels and Dalhousie.

The King raised his hand for quiet. When the noise abated, he said, "We have information from elsewhere. Sir Walter?"

Broad-shouldered and deep-chested, Walter Haliburton was every bit a Scottish warrior, but his face was drawn. He stepped onto the dais so he could be seen. "It hit Dirleton like a storm. Three of my men-at-arms are seized with it and —" His voice broke. "—my daughter has it as well. When I left, they still lived. I dinnae ken if they still do."

"I have a question of the bishop, Your Grace," I said, pushing through the crowd. "Reverence, I have heard that the cooler weather in the north may lessen the deaths. Was that the case when we suffered it before?"

The bishop put his hands together as though at prayer and pressed the fingers to his lips. After a moment, he said, "We suffered only a few deaths in Saint Andrews. Whether it was our prayers and God's mercy or that something about the coolness of the weather kept the evil away..." He shook his head. "That I dinnae ken."

"The Danes had it, and it is cold enough there," said Haliburton.

"Still, it seems to me that it is worth going north." I wanted Wilikyn out of Edinburgh if there was even a chance it would protect him. "To Saint Andrews or Dunfermline Palace mayhap. At the least, it would be farther than the present contagion." I would gladly face any man with a weapon, but I had no shame at fleeing from the great plague.

"All of us here saw the horrors of it." The reality of it was sickening. We had seen strong men drop of it right in front of us. We had buried entire families. "To protect the kingdom's governance, I believe the King must go north and as many as possible with him."

"Your Grace," the seneschal bowed to David, "my staff is well accustomed to preparing for you to travel so all could be readied in three days."

"I think we havenae choice. We shall depart for Saint Andrews as soon as possible." David looked grim. He must have seen the horrors when he was in England, even as a prisoner. "Maister Hogg, could you inform the other burgesses and spread word to the guildmaisters? I must know and decide what to do. Even Perth might be safer than Edinburgh for now."

"Am I still to send my men to bring the Earl of Mar to you, Your Grace? This seems more urgent."

"Put it off until we are at Saint Andrews. He was at Kildrummy Castle a few days ago to keep out of my sight. Once we are there, I want him brought before me." The King grimaced. "I mean to teach him a lesson to cease his extortions. I warned him." It was widely known that Thomas of Mar was deeply in debt and exceeding his rights to raise taxes to try to pay them, but I had not realized that the King had had enough.

Haliburton made obeisance to the king. "Sire, I must return to Dirlton since I have given you warning. I cannae abandon my family."

"Of course, Sir Walter." The King rose. "The rest have preparations to make, so the meeting is dismissed."

Everyone broke into separate discussions, and the seneschal scurried out the rear door of the hall to set the servants to work. Will pulled me aside. "You must tell me if I can help. Leaving with a bairn will complicate things."

I scratched my forehead. That was indeed a complication. He could not travel without his wet nurse as well. "His wet nurse cannae be expected to ride. There will be wains to carry the king's goods and litters for some of the ladies. It will be a longer ride than some could make by horse." I patted his shoulder. "I have it in hand."

Leaving with so many people always took longer than it should to bring order out of confusion, so when there was no sign of Will as our long caravan clattered through Netherbow Gate, I thought nothing of it. Normally we kept each other company to break the monotony of the road, but he had his own men to see to. Eventually, he would find me. Wilikyn kept me entertained, holding onto the side of the wain, babbling and pointing. Every bird was a subject of wonder. My future wife rode beside me, and we chatted for a time. I was pleased she preferred riding to being hauled in a litter. But when we stopped to rest the animals, there was no still sign of Will. No one had seen him, not even his serjeant, who had assumed his maister was riding with the lords. Something had to be wrong. I put James in command of my men, told the wet nurse I would return shortly, and turned back. By myself, it would only be an hour's ride.

Edinburgh was eerily quiet, and only a few men-at-arms had been left behind to patrol the castle walls. The bells were ringing for None, the afternoon shadows draped across the bailey when I strode into the keep. The thud of my boots on the stone floor raised goosebumps up the back of my neck. I hurried up the stairs and opened the door, calling, "Will?"

Fully clothed, he lay stretched on the bed with no drapes

because he had brought none. His arm was thrown across his eyes.

"Will?" I froze at the door, unsure what might be wrong.

He moved his arm and turned his head. His face was flushed and slick with sweat. He pushed himself up on an elbow. "You should be gone, Archie. What are you doing here?"

"What do you think?" I swallowed the fear that gripped my throat. "What—"

"You ken what!" His eyes flared with temper for a moment, but then he flopped flat on the bed. "I was alright this morning, just a bit feverish." The sound he made was meant to be a laugh. "But the soreness started in my armpit. The sore isnae large yet. But it will be."

I opened my mouth to ask if he was sure, but of course, he was. We had both seen the signs too many times in the last plague year for there to be any doubt. We had escaped last time and lived through battles where thousands had died. That he would be taken now... My mind refused to grasp it.

"Go on." His voice was tight, as though he had to force the words. "Catch up with the others. There is naught you can do here."

"God damn it," I picked up a stool in the corner and slammed it next to his bed. "If you think I will go off and leave you..." I poured some water from a pitcher on the small table into a pewter cup and set it on the stool. It was all I could think to do. "You cannae think that."

He barked another laugh. "Do you think that will help?"

"Where is your poxy squire? Why are you lying in your clothes?"

"I sent him away, Archie. If he hasnae caught it, then better he left."

"Och, then I suppose I play squire. You had better hope I remember how." When I started unbuttoning his doublet, he batted at my hand, but not hard enough to stop me. He was not that weak yet, just thought he had to protest. I tried not to look at the darkening bubo under his arm when I worked him out of it, but I had felt his wince from the pain. Once he was undressed, I jerked the coverlet over him. "I have heard of people surviving." Sweat had soaked his hair while I moved him about.

He snorted. "So have I. I even met one or two of them." He gave a long, silent look. "There is something you can do for me, Archie. I dinnae want to die unshriven. Do you ken...? Might there still be a priest at the chapel—" he grimaced. "—one nae afraid to come to give me the Last Rites?"

"None was ringing, so there had to be someone at the chapel." I clenched my teeth. "He will give you the rites. Dinnae fash."

When I turned for the door, he said, "After you send him, get you gone. You have a wee lad to care for. There isnae more you can do for me."

____

CHAPTER EIGHTEEN

____

After unbuckling my sword belt and propping my sword by the heavy wooden door, I stepped inside the chapel. The scent of incense and beeswax was a comfort, as was the sight of the priest kneeling in prayer in the colored light of the stained-glass window beyond the altar.

I waited a moment, hesitating to interrupt his prayers but afraid to delay, and cleared my throat.

He jerked and rose to his feet, eyebrows raised in surprise. "I thought all the knights had left." He seemed an ordinary man, a little pudgy with his brown hair tonsured.

"I need you to come. My friend wants the Last Rites."

His chest rose and fell with a deep breath, and he squared his shoulders. "The plague? Already?"

"I fear he carried it with him." If I had to, I would drag him. If Will died, he would not die unshriven.

He must have seen something in my face because he raised his hand and patted the air as though to calm me. "That is why I stayed." He stooped and picked up a leather bag. It took only a moment to fill it with what he needed. It took only minutes to return to the keep.

A look of relief passed over Will's face when he saw the priest. I told them I would return shortly and closed the door. Whatever he might confess was no business of mine. To my surprise, a couple of servants sat in the kitchen at a long, scarred table munching on bread, cheese, and capons. I asked them why they had not fled, but the older man shrugged and said there was nowhere they could run. The younger helped me fill a pitcher with ale and put it on a tray with some of the bread and half of one of the capons. When I carried it into the bedchamber, the priest sat on the edge of the bed and nodded to me.

Will scowled. "Did I nae tell you to get your gone? Whether I live or die, there isnae more you can do."

I set the tray on the stool where Will could reach it. "You really expect me to leave you here alone?"

"I shall keep an eye on him and do what I can." The priest stood. "I will call on you in the morning, Sir William."

He gave us his blessing and strode purposefully into the hall. I wondered how many others he needed to visit to give them some last comfort.

Will propped himself up on his elbow. "I mean it, Archie. Your son needs you."

My stomach twisted.

"My old friend, remember me in your prayers." He lay back down, pulled the coverlet up to his shoulders, and turned his back. "Now go."

"Will..." I could barely remember a time when he was not my closest friend. My companion-in-arms. I could not count the times he had saved me from death or capture. "Will, I am staying."

It was the hardest thing I had ever done, sitting beside him as he suffered. He struggled so hard not to moan or cry out in pain when I wiped away the blood and pus that drained out of the sores. I held him up as I dribbled water between his cracked lips, but he vomited it back up. He shook with chills no matter how many the covers. When he was finally still and I realized he was gone, I would not weep. He would have shamed me. I just called the priest and prayed at his graveside.

It was not until I was riding in the fading light of the gloaming on the road to Saint Andrews that I let the tears fall.

CHAPTER NINETEEN

Early August 1361

It had soon been decided that the King and his closest advisers would be more comfortable at the castle of John de Pilmuir, Bishop of Mora, in Spyvie, although the bishop was too frail to leave his bed. He was a wizened, tottering old man already, the few times I had seen him, at least in his eighties. Instead, Alexander Bur, the bishop's archdeacon, and Bishop de Landallis would act as our hosts. It was as wet as you would expect for a Scottish September.

Archdeacon Bur met the King and me as we descended from our bedchambers. He was a tall, lean person with a serious mien but he had on occasion been very kind to me.

He made obeisance to the David. "Bishop de Landallis has taken possession of Bishop de Pilmuir's closet, Your Grace. I was about to send you word that some new message just came that he wishes to share with you. And you as well, Sir Archibald."

The King smiled and thanked him. Bur had been at Château Gaillard with us when we were children, though I barely knew him then. But he had been a good friend of the king, despite already being a priest.

"God bless you," he said, passing into the wet afternoon.

Bishop de Landallis rose when the King and I entered. Today he wore his everyday black cassock with red buttons down the front and a red sash. The fine fuzz of white hair around his tonsure would better suit a less powerful man. He went to the door and told the hovering servant, "Bring some wine and some of those honeyed apple tarts."

Apples had just ripened on the trees and the bishop seemed to favor them. King David took a seat at the small table and the bishop and I followed. In a moment, the room was in motion as platters of tarts, a flagon of wine, and silver goblets were laid on the table and the fire built up to ward off the chill of the damp autumn afternoon.

"I shall see to serving myself," he said, and the servants scurried away.

He picked up a document with a large, be-ringed hand and gave a sigh of satisfaction. From it hung the papal seal. It always surprised me that it was so modest, not even a finger's length in size with the head of Saints Peter and Paul with a cross between them. The parchment was covered with styl-ized and complex verbiage in Latin. Whatever it said had the bishop looking like a cat with a dish of rich cream.

He inclined his head and said, "Good news from the pope. The dispensation for your marriage has arrived."

David chuckled softly and poured himself a goblet of the wine. "That will put Robert Stewart in a fury." He lifted his cup to me. "Nor will your cousin be pleased to see you gain so much power."

I poured a goblet for the bishop and one for me. "They had every chance to stop me." I clinked my goblet to the king's. "It isnae my fault Robert Stewart is a coward and the man he hired couldnae fight."

The bishop sipped the excellent claret and said, "I should wed you to the lady as soon as possible."

It was midafternoon, and the watery sunlight was beginning to fade. The flames in the fragrant beeswax candles shivered and then stilled. It began to rain and droplets of water ran down the glass windowpanes like the tears I could not shed. Will would not be there to join in the celebration.

"Has any more news about the situation in France arrived with that dispensation?" the King asked.

"The French have fallen even further behind on King Jean's ransom." His smile was wry since David had just stopped paying on his own ransom, sure the English would be in no hurry to attack. "And everyone says King Jean is failing. He willnae live long. When the Dauphin Charles is king..."

The King scowled. Clearly, he considered this bad news, although even with a new and young king, the French would be in no better state to fight the English than they were now. The English had laid waste to most of France and taken much of it for their own in the Treaty of Brétigny. If the treaty broke down, they would start fighting again. As always, the busier the English were fighting the French, the less likely they were to attack us. I had time to consider it as the King studied the goblet in his hand, and the bishop cocked his head, watching the king.

"Your Grace," the bishop said, "why the scowl?"

"If the war in France starts up again, the English will need my ransom to help pay the costs. They ignore that I am nae paying it for now and we negotiate still. John of Gaunt's father-in-law has died, you ken, so my representatives can use that to their advantage."

Behind the bishop, a tapestry wrinkled in a draft, and Salome seemed to smirk as she offered up the head of John the Baptist.

I set my goblet down hard. "Parliament will never accept Prince John as your heir or your giving land to the men who backed the pretender."

He raised an eyebrow and glared at me, trying to stare me down.

I stared back. "Twice you have tried to name an English heir, and it only weakened you each time." I leaned slightly toward him and softened my tone. A King rarely reacted well to a raised voice. "You have gained too much this last year to risk angering your supporters. If Douglas and Stewart rebel, as I believe they will, you have the strength and backing to put them down hard. I beg you dinnae risk that."

"And Dunbar will be right beside them." The bishop nodded. "Sir Archibald may have a point."

David sniffed. "Robert Stewart is too much of a coward to stand up to me. He will run just as he did at Neville's Cross. As he forced you to do, Archie, after you took Berwick-upon-Tweed."

"My cousin willnae run. As old and sleekit as he is, I dinnae think Dunbar will either. He isnae a coward despite running at Neville's Cross." I spread my hands. "You ken I am your man, whatever you do, but such an agreement would only weaken us when we cannae afford it." That the Earls of Douglas, Strathearn, Dunbar, and Mar were not with the king's court was notable. Of course, the King had not invited them to join us either, so they must have retreated from the great plague to their own lands in the north.

The King intended a renewed and strengthened monarchy as his father had bequeathed him to be his monu-ment, a living and breathing one long after he was gone. For that, he needed an heir to undermine the strength of the magnates, especially Stewart, Douglas, and Dunbar. No wonder he had glared at me. He hated even the hint that Robert Stewart, whom he despised, would succeed him. And he hated that he had in the past had to bend to the power of Douglas and Dunbar.

"Now we need to prod the Queen into announcing that

she is taking vows," the bishop said. "Once you are remarried, it cuts the ground under the Stewarts as your heirs."

"With the plague still raging, it is hard to do so. I would go to England myself if not for that." We had news that the Earl of Angus had died of the plague in his dungeon along with countless thousands of others across the south of Scotland. So far, it had not reached this far north. Once winter hit, we should be safe, but would winter arrive in time?

"Now, about Archie's wedding, we must have the bans read." The bishop tapped his lips. "The feast will lack some of the usual exuberance as we will hold it here in my home, but what matters is that it will be done."

I pressed my lips together to keep from smirking. Apparently, the good bishop would not allow me to be stripped of my clothes amongst raucous jests and thrown naked into my marriage bed. But he was right about one thing. What would matter was that the lady of Bothwell and I would be wed.

CHAPTER TWENTY

Late August 1361

"Joanna de Moravia, I take you to my wedded wife, for fair or for foul, in sickness and in health, until death us depart, and thereto I plight you my troth."

Behind us, Wilikyn babbled, "Da! Da!" He sounded insulted at receiving none of my attention. Several giggles and a few tuts came from onlookers as his wet nurse shushed him. Joanna glanced toward him. Her mouth twitched with amusement, but Bishop de Landallis cleared his throat so she ducked her head and gave her vow.

The bishop accepted a broad gold band set with an emerald that I held out to him. He blessed it and gave it back. Joanna's hand was perfectly steady when I took it in mine.

"With this ring, I thee wed: This gold I thee give, with my body I thee worship, and with all my worldly goods I thee endow." I slipped the ring a little way onto each finger, saying, "In the name of the Father, the Son, and the Holy Spirit." With the last phrase, I slipped it all the way onto her ring finger. I wondered if it occurred to Joanna as it did to me that she was the one with worldly goods to endow. My part would be guarding them.

De Landallis raised his voice so that his closing blessing rose above the cheers. Joanna tossed silver pennies to the crowd, scooped up by the servants and men-at-arms mixed in the crowd.

I held out my hand out, and she placed hers on it. A piper and drummer stuck up a jaunty tune, and the bishop motioned for me to follow to his door, only a short stroll down the cobble street.

David slapped me on the back. "Lead the way, Archie!" He tucked Margaret Drummond's hand on his elbow with a fond look. I could not see the attraction. She must have been thirty, so not young, and pretty enough, but no more than half a dozen other women I knew. Perhaps her attraction was that she had given birth to a son. She was sharp-eyed and honey-tongued, and I could not trust her. But the King did.

I smiled at my bride and stopped to give my son a quick ruffle of his dark hair before the wet nurse took him to their bedchamber. We strolled ahead of the chattering crowd, but how I wished Will was here with one of his jests. No doubt it would not be the last time I thought that, but it would be wrong to darken our wedding day, so I let the music pull us along. Who were not here were the earls of Dunbar, Douglas and Strathearn. Oddly, Thomas, Earl of Mar, was also missing. The King, the bishop, and Alexander Bur followed directly behind us with a crowd of others, including Joanna's mother, John de Menteith, who rarely came to court as her health was weak. A somewhat subdued crowd fell in behind, chattering and laughing, but foregoing the usual ribald jests. When offended, the bishop had a severe glare.

A guard in the King's livery opened the door for us. Etienne and Jacquet above in a small gallery strummed their instruments as we entered. Sunlight flooded across the hall.

Trestle tables draped in white cloths were set with gleaming pewter goblets and trenchers. Servants scurried to serve the wine.

"I am glad it willnae be too raucous a feast," Joanna whispered. "I had such at my first wedding. It was merry, but once was enough."

Squeezing her hand, I said, "I am glad you dinnae mind." I guided her past the fifty guests onto the dais, standing next to the king.

Bishop de Landallis' blessing stretched unnecessarily long, but at last, he made the sign of the cross, and the King raised his wine cup. "To the bride and groom!" Everyone grabbed their cups, shouting and cheering, and drained them.

The trumpets blasted to announce servers carrying in platters of baked lamprey in wine, roast swan in ginger sauce, and the bishop's favorite apple tarts basted with honey. Joanna took a bite of the breast of swan from my fingers and laid her hand on my arm.

The melody from the minstrel's gallery changed to *Douce Dame Jolie* and Perrette's singing accompanied her brothers.

The minstrels changed to *Vos Qui Admiramini* and other French tunes I did not recognize. Another course came. Joanna leaned against my shoulder and whispered, "The minstrels are very good, but when I welcomed that it wouldnae be raucous, mayhap I meant a little more raucous than this."

I had to agree. "When you are in your own hall, you may do it however you want." I chuckled. "With nae advice from the bishop."

"Even for a bishop, His Reverence is a bit staid." She popped a bit of burrebrede in her mouth. "But he does have talented cooks. I dinnae suppose we could steal one away?"

"For you, anything, my lady. Even risking excommunication."

She tittered and ate another bite of the baked sweet.

A squire in the king's livery peeped through the rear door, biting his lower lip. He scurried to the King and knelt to hand him a message. I took a sip of my wine, watching from the corner of my eye as David broke the seal and read the contents. Delivering a message at a wedding feast was well beyond what was allowed.

He leaned back, took a drink of his wine, and read it again. After refolding it, he handed it to Bishop de Landallis. When he looked my way, I raised my eyebrows. He motioned me closer and whispered, "The queen is dead." He frowned. "But a wedding feast isnae time to announce it."

People had noticed that something was going on. I realized my mouth was open and snapped it shut. She had been only about forty years old. It must have been the plague.

"What's wrong?" Joanna asked in a low voice.

I tipped my head toward the people who were staring. "I will tell you privily. It would be best if we act as though nothing has happened."

She frowned at being denied, but nibbled at a piece of capon.

When the last course was down to a few crumbs on the trenchers, Joanna's mother, thin and frail, leaned forward. "It's time, my dear."

Cheers rang across the hall, and everyone raised their cup. Joanna's face was rosy with blushes. She curtsied to the King and bishop, turned, and accompanied her mother into the passage to the bedchambers.

James leaned to yell down the table, "What are you waiting for, Archie?"

The bishop stood and glared at my cousin. "Remember that this is the house of a bishop. I shall havenae lewd behavior."

The King laughed and shook his head, but obediently he,

James, Preston and a dozen other men escorted me to the bedchamber door.

James bumped me with his shoulder. "The bishop fears we might break something, but I dinnae ken what." Everyone laughed. Joanna's mother nodded to indicate that Joanna was waiting and exited.

The King shoved me inside and proclaimed, "I shall expect a report from the lady on the morrow that you did your duty." They were still laughing when I slammed the door in their faces.

Joanna was kneeling on the bed, the coverlet pulled up to her bare breasts. "Now, tell me what happened."

I started unbuttoning my doublet. "The letter, I dinnae ken from whom, said that Queen Joan is dead."

Her eyes widened, and she put her hand to her chest. "Poor lady! He wasnae always kind, I fear."

"Aye. They both tried at least to like each other, I think, and then gave up." After I kicked off my shoes and stripped out of my hose, I slid into bed. "He was surprised, but I dinnae think very grieved."

She made a sound of agreement. Her hair fell in waves over her shoulders and down her back. I had never seen it loose before. It was dark brown with a shimmer of red, almost the color of cherrywood. It suited her fair complexion and the few freckles that dotted her nose. I wound a strand around my finger.

"I wasnae keeping it secret, but our reactions were causing talk, and the King wanted to wait to announce it. He said a wedding feast wasnae the place."

"I suppose, although everyone saw that something had happened." She shifted so she could pillow her head on my shoulder. I kissed her forehead. She was soft and yielding against my side.

"I will do my best to see that you never regret our

marriage, Joanna. I swear it by all that is holy." I stroked her breast, cupping it so the warm flesh filled my hand. She turned so I could kiss her. After a moment, she opened her lips for me.

I drew her against me to enjoy the warmth of her flesh, kissing her neck and down her shoulder. She gave a little gasp. Once more, I took her mouth with mine. Her arms encircled my neck and snuggled against me. I took my time, for both our sakes, stroking and exploring. When we came together, the rhythms of our bodies joined and matched.

Afterward, she sighed softly, twirling a piece of the black pelt on my chest which made me smile. Outside, a nightingale trilled a song. Her breathing slowed as she dropped off to sleep. We had much to learn of each other, but tonight what we had was enough.

When the morning sun spilled through the shutters, I stroked Joanna's hair as she rested her head on my shoulder. The King had done better than he might have imagined in choosing me a wife and for more than some baronies, important as they were.

I had almost drifted off again when there was a knock on the door. "my lord," Gil said.

I sighed. "What is it?"

Gil opened the door a crack and stuck in his head. "The King requires your presence." He opened the door wider. "He is in a raging temper, so you may want to hurry. Shall I help you dress?"

"Go tell His Grace I will be there shortly."

He looked doubtful at the idea of returning to David without me, but I waved him away.

Joanna sat up, letting the coverlet fall to her lap. "Announcing Queen Joan's death cannae be put off, but that wouldnae put him in a temper."

"Aye, you are right."

As I approached the great hall's rear door, the King shouted, "Then where is the scurvy plague-sore?"

I stepped through the rear door to find the King glowering at the lord marischal as James and Haliburton hurried through the main door.

"The Kildrummy chamberlain said the earl left for Leith two weeks past, planning to take a ship to France to fight with the English." The marischal threw up his hands. "Even if we took the risk to send my men to Leith where there is the plague, he will have already fled."

David folded his arms and frowned at the floor. "If I cannae reach him, I can reach what he values." He lifted his gaze to the marischal. "We will raise what army we can here in the north as quickly as possible. I mean to take Thomas's Kildrummy Castle. That will bring my cousin to his senses."

"Kildrummy Castle isnae an easy castle to take," I said.

"Och, it willnae be so hard." David shrugged. "We will lay siege, nae attack it. Many of the crops are still being harvested, so food will be in short supply. Foreby, my cousin will ken that I will forgive him eventually—when he comes to his senses. Anyone else holding out when I demand surrender willnae be so sure."

It was no surprise when the frail and elderly Bishop de Pilmuir died only a few days after our wedding as we prepared to lay siege to Kildrummy. The canons of the Moray bishopric gathered, and David, having made it very clear that Alexander Bur was his choice for bishop, voted him as their choice. Of course, he had been archdeacon for some years, so maybe they really did prefer him, or maybe having a king on the spot decided them. The final decision would be the pope's, but there was little likelihood he would oppose their choice. In the meantime, Alexander Bur would act as bishop.

CHAPTER TWENTY-ONE

September 1361, near Kildrummy Castle

The enormous, red stone fortress of Kildrummy Castle rose at the top of a steep slope. It was oddly shaped like a shield, with the wide part overlooking a high cliff impossible to climb. The front was a massive twin-towered gatehouse that I looked at enviously. I added it to a secret list of what I would want in a castle of my own. Of course, the drawbridge was raised.

Overhead, my Douglas banner snapped in a strong, late-summer wind. Behind me rode my cousin James and with him rode Andrew, Thomas, and Nicholas Erskine, followed by the seventy-five men-at-arms I had brought from Edinburgh Castle. It was a weaker force than I would have liked, but with the plague, raising more men from my newly acquired baronies was impossible.

Rigs covered with golden barley were ready for harvest but were empty of people to do it. Our coming had been heralded by clouds of choking dust on the dry dirt roads and no doubt by men running or riding frantically ahead to give warning. But the King had given strict commands that the people and their crops were not to be touched nor their goods stolen. It was his cousin, the earl he meant to punish. Of course, they had no way of knowing that, and a herschip, burning everything in sight, had ofttimes been a king's method of bringing a rebellious noble to heel. The houses were empty as well, my scouts reported. That meant they had been admitted to the castle, where they would quickly eat through food supplies. It seemed that King David was right.

We followed the force of the King and the lord marischal at enough distance not to choke on the cloud of dust that they raised in their passing. Already they were spreading out to camp at the base of the sharp slope. The castle was poised like a great stone ship about to plunge its bow down the slope, crushing all in its way. Golden sunlight flooded its red sandstone walls and towers. Now to take it...

Crossbowmen moved along the parapet walk. Above the gatehouse streamed the blue banner with the gold cross fitchée of the Earl of Mar. My column streamed to the edge of the camp where the king's several hundred men were setting up camp. Already his pavilion was raised, and the gold Lion Rampant banner was planted on a tall pole.

I dismounted just to the right of where they were making camp and ordered the men to do the same.

"my lord," Gil asked, "where should we raise your pavilion?"

I pointed. "On that side of the king's camp." After he nodded, I went on, "Baggage and supplies on the right side. Horse lines beyond that." It would be best to have our own. It at least cut down on the stench that built up in a camp.

"Remember to put the latrine pit well back." James snorted. "But not so far back that if the men have too much ale, they won't be willing to stumble to it in the dark. We may be here for a while."

"I dinnae ken that we will have enough ale for that to be a problem. We can hunt meat." I had seen plenty of signs of game, including a fine stag at the top of a hill, and hunting would break the monotony of a siege besides providing food.

Dipping his head toward the village, Colbyn said, "If some people fled to the woods instead of the castle, we might be able to buy supplies."

"It is possible, I suppose. Meanwhile, you assign sentries." I squinted at the fortress, which I knew only by reputation, having never had a reason to go there. "I suppose there is a postern gate. Anyone ken where it is or the layout inside?"

They all shrugged in ignorance.

"You all ken what to do. I dinnae need to stand over you." I brushed some of the thick coating of dust from my sleeves and doublet. "I had best go report to the king."

James said, "I hope he can convince them to surrender. I dinnae want to have to climb those walls."

I had to agree. The walls were at least twenty-five feet high, and numerous crossbows poked out between the merlons to show a large number of defenders. I paused to watch a score of the lord marischal's men hammering rough-cut wood into a barrier across the road down from the draw-bridge, out of range of the crossbows. I doubted they would dare attack the king, but if they did, at least the barrier would slow down a charge.

When I reached his large pavilion, I called out a greeting, and the King told me to enter. He sat on a folding camp bench, elbows on his knees, his hands relaxed. I bowed.

The marischal crossed his arms, frowning toward the castle as though he could see it through the canvas. "The people fleeing our approach must have doubled the number of mouths to feed."

"And he will be counting how many days their food will last," I said. "I assume there is a well?"

"Aye, there is," the King said. "I have visited the castle many times. The constable will be in charge. A tough fighter, but I doubt this is a situation he kens how to deal with. I must speak with him." He walked to the small table where a flagon and several pewter cups sat beside an unlit candle. "Reginald, send a herald to invite him to speak to me. I will meet him at the foot of the drawbridge."

I frowned. "But you would be within range of a bowshot."

David stroked his pointed beard, smiling. "Then the two of you had better accompany me to confuse them as to who they need to aim at."

"What?" the lord marischal exclaimed.

David chuckled. "I jest. They arenae going to risk attacking me under a flag or truce. Have the herald give my word that we willnae attack. At least, not yet."

Andrew Erskine carried our white flag of truce as we trotted up the road past the half-built barrier. A crossbow poked out from between each merlon. A crossbow bolt might penetrate my plate, but I hoped not. We pulled up and waited as the drawbridge dropped and a small side gate opened so the portcullis would not have to be raised.

The constable rode through, his horse's hooves thudding on the wooden bridge. He stopped halfway to us. His chainmail was polished to a sheen, his helm open to show dark eyebrows in a long, narrow face.

He bowed his head to the king, but his blue eyes slid sideways from the King to the marischal, then to me, and back to the King again.

"You will surrender the castle to me," the King said.

"I cannae. My lord left it in my care," he said, his words accented with the rounded vowels of a Gaelic speaker. "It is my duty to hold it until his return."

I twitched when David nudged his mount with a knee,

and it took a step closer to the man. David raised his chin and leaned forward to stare into the constable's face. "The castle is now mine. I have seized it for the crown for Thomas's crimes."

The black brows drew together. "I willnae betray my liege lord."

David raised an imperious hand. "I am nae here to debate. Your lord is sworn to my service. As he owes me obedience, so do you." He let his hand drop and said in a milder tone, "I respect your loyalty to my cousin, so I grant you one week. That will show that you held his castle for him and absolve you of blame. Then you surrender it, or I take it. And if you force me to violence, I promise you that you will hang as a traitor to your rightful Lord King."

David wheeled his mount and rode toward the camp, never once looking back. I turned my horse's head and followed him toward the siege line. My back itched from the eyes of the crossbowmen on the ramparts.

Back at the camp, I swung from the saddle, and Gil took the reins.

"How did it go?" said James.

I looked back toward the fortress as the drawbridge gradually raised. "His Grace gave them a powerful message. I hope they heard it."

Laying siege is always boring. Men tended their armor and weapons and practiced with swords and spears. Whoever could sing, and some who could not, tried to entertain each other. The men were not allowed to stray far from camp but hunted hares and pigeons nearby for the cook pot.

David said there were better things to do than sit in camp, so he left the lord marischal in charge, and we rode to Aberdeen, where he had business. He confirmed Cunningham of Kilmaurs as guardian of Carrick, which was sure to enrage Robert Stewart, and granted lands to William

Livingston. To my shock, he named me to replace the Earl of Douglas as Warden of the Western March. My heart drummed in my chest, and I bent a knee to him with a wide grin. We spent four nights as luxurious guests of the Bishop of Aberdeen. The next day, we returned to Kildrummy. The marischal assured us that all had been quiet in our absence, and after the day-long ride, I was ready to throw myself down on my cot.

At the first light of day, Gil handed me a bannock still warm from the fire and pondered the fortress. If they did not surrender, it would mean mustering more men for an assault. When the pole holding the Mar banner aloft tilted and slowly fell, I laughed with delight. Then I sprinted to tell the king.

He slapped me on the shoulder and said he had told us so. After naming Walter Moigne as guardian of the castle, we rode for Spyvie Castle.

CHAPTER TWENTY-TWO

December 1361

There were preparations needed for Advent and the Christmas celebrations, so Bishop de Landallis left for his own bishopric of Saint Andrews, to the relief of many of us. Not that he was disliked, but he was judgmental and moralistic when it came to more raucous celebrations. As an archdeacon, the now Bishop Bur had been known to smile and even take part.

Word came from below the Forth that the plague still raged, though it had not reached us. The roads were closed, and only a few ships were allowed to land, but the crews were not allowed ashore. Every day at the mass, we prayed for the dead and to spare ourselves from the ravages. There was no mention of possibly returning to Edinburgh.

Snow set in, and it was possible to forget any worries in the great hall before a roaring fire. William was learning to toddle and delighted in being propped on my knee to be bounced to a pony rhyme that came to me from a cloudy memory. His loud laughter made everyone smile. Joanna sometimes gave him a sweet and seemed to grow fond of him.

The three days a week of fasting during Advent seemed

like little hardship. There were salmons cooked with leeks, eel in saffron sauce, spicy pea soups, apples and raisins, and apple tarts.

Christmas was the best I could remember in many years. From the pre-dawn mass, we went to the great hall, where wine flowed like water, and the feasting lasted for days. Whole roast pigs were paraded out, roast venison basted with honey, pigeon pies, gingerbreads, and blancmange. Wilikyn's wet nurse put a stop to his taking part when he threw up on the king. David laughed, and one of the Haliburton squires wiped up the mess. Halfway through the twelve days of celebration on the Feast of Fools, even Bishop Bur took part and allowed a lowly subdeacon to deliver the homily at mass.

On Twelfth Night, we drank and feasted one last day. I awakened the next day, knowing that we would again face reality.

CHAPTER TWENTY-THREE

Early March 1362, Edinburgh Castle

"I am sorry, Your Grace. I am merely delivering what news I ken."

The man-at-arms shuffled his feet and nervously wiped his hands on his surcoat. King David ground his teeth, his face apoplectic. The great hall was filled with a pregnant silence.

"Walter Haliburton is a prisoner, you say?"

"I was returning from Aberlady, where my lord had sent me on an errand," he said in a rush to get the bad news over. "And attackers were flying the banner of the Earl of Douglas. I waited until nightfall and sneaked into the castle town, and the alewife hid me in her brewhouse. That night I heard some of their men bragging that their lord ordered him thrown in a dungeon."

"What?" The king's frown became a black scowl. "The dared to attack the castle? You should have told me that first!"

"I... I..." The man contorted his face and backed up a step.

I grimaced. This had been long coming, but at last, it was here. Open civil war. David glanced my way, and I nodded. I would summon all the knights who had joined my following and decide how many of my men-at-arms must remain here to defend the burgh and the castle. I would have the wet nurse bring my son into the castle and assign them a chamber. The rebels were unlikely to attack Edinburgh, but I would take no chances. There was a long list of the King's loyal men. Many were here, most importantly lord marischal, but more would have to be summoned.

As usual, word was quickly spreading in the castle that something was afoot, and the hall was filling. Joanna came to stand next to me, chewing her lip and her hands tightly clasped. From across the hall, James nodded to me.

"Did they say if Sir Walter was injured? What about his family?"

"They didnae say, only that he loudly protested upon being thrust into the dungeon." His face glistened with sweat. "I hid the night and sneaked away at first light, but I couldnae make good time on a horse that had ridden so far. I brought the news as soon as I could." He twisted his hands together. "I swear, Sire."

It had logic to it, and the King moved on. "Could you tell how many men they had?"

"I dared nae get close enough to count them. It was an escalade. I saw them climbing the ladders and fighting on the ramparts. There were enough that the fight was soon over. I wanted to help but thought bringing you word of the treachery was more important."

Haliburton must have had about a hundred men to defend Dirleton Castle. To defeat them so readily, my cousin must have brought several times that many men. To retake the castle, we would need... I chewed my lip as I tried to calculate the number, but it would depend on how many the Douglas left because I was sure he would not remain to defend it.

Instead, he would move fast to attack another castle, trying to weaken the King before we could strike back.

"There you were right." He dismissed the man. Fingers tapping on the arm of his throne, he seemed to gather himself. After a few moments, during which no one dared speak, he asked, "Archie, how many men can you raise?"

"I can take seventy-five men-at-arms and archers from the castle and still leave it well-defended." I squinted as I considered how many men were at my castles, Joanna's castles that were now mine, that would be within a day's march. Between the plague and seizing Kildrummy Castle, there had been no chance to visit them since our wedding, but I had a good idea how many men each had. Only the ones in Lanark or near it were close enough for its men to reach us quickly. "I can send for twenty-five from Drumsagard Castle without stripping it of defenses. Avondale and Lurdenlaw can each send twenty. They can meet us while we march or, at worst, when we reach Dirleton."

"Then do so."

The lord marischal cleared his throat. "I have fifty men-at-arms with me." He looked up at the ceiling, his lips moving like he was counting. "Erskine, Cockburn, Campbell, More, Scrymgeour, and Lindsay should have between a dozen and a score men-at-arms that can ride with them. Robert Ramsay of Forfar, the Leslies, and Maurice Drummond might have more. They usually have twoscore in their tail."

The King steepled his fingers and pressed them to his lips. "Send word to meet us at Dirleton and nae to delay to raise more. The payment for their men will come from the royal treasury." He stood. "We will march at Terce, so we all have work to do."

CHAPTER TWENTY-FOUR

The Next Night, Dirleton Castle

The Next Night

A brisk wind was blowing away from the castle, taking any sound that might give away our presence. The clouds cut off even the starlight, so the castle was nothing more than an even blacker hulk against a black sky with only hints of light through the arrow slots in the towers.

The lord marischal asked, "How deep is the moat?"

"I am told only a little deeper than a man's height, so we can make it across. Just a matter of holding our breaths." I wiped drops of water off my face. "We will be only a little wetter than we already are."

"They have to expect a counterattack," the King said.

"Aye. But it is late and wet. Men get tired and sloppy. And they will not expect us to arrive so quickly." I pretended not to be nervous and pasted on a smile even though they could not see it in the dark. This was a risky tactic. Lifting a rope ladder on a spear to catch the grappling hook on the parapet was an old trick. It worked as long as the walls were not higher than a man could reach overhead with a spear. And if the enemy did not know you were coming.

"Are you sure you dinnae want me to be part of the climbing party?" the marischal said. He was in command under the king, but since he had never made an escalade was leaving the planning to me.

"Just be ready to charge as soon as we open the gate." I started to add and lead the retreat if it all went wrong, but that was a thought I did not want to put into my men's minds.

"We shall be," the King said.

My hands were wet with sweat. I wiped my hands on my surcoat, pulled it over my head, and started removing my armor to the quilted arming doublet.

Under his breath, James muttered I was crazy. Henry Ashkirk replied he hoped not. There was a clatter as the twoscore men-at-arms stripped to their arming doublets and hose that protected them from being scraped by armor. The quilting would be little protection from a sword blow or an arrow, so we needed to kill the guards before they even realized they were under attack.

Dirleton did not have a drawbridge but a wooden ramp from this side of the moat up to the keep's door. It could easily be cast down in case of attack. However, it had an outer and inner portcullis that would have to be raised before the King and the lord marischal led in the main force.

David huffed a false laugh, but he had never led an escalade before. "They say both of our fathers once crossed a moat naked. I wonder if that is true."

"Aye, well, I would rather not." I hunch-walked down the line of men, slapping a man here and there on the shoulder and muttering a little encouragement as I checked to be sure they were as ready as I could make them. I hefted one of the rope ladders over my shoulder, picked up a spear, and said, "Remember, silent as a ghost." My skin twitched at going into a fight with no sword on my hip.

I was proud of my men. Not one had questioned being told to cross a moat with water over their heads or asked what they were doing leaving their armor behind. But we would win. I was sure, but at what cost?

I sat on the edge of the moat and slid into the water. There were a few splashes as my men followed. I froze, my heart pounding like a smith's hammer, but the only sound was the soft patter of the rain. The water was icy cold, but only up to my chest. I took a step, feeling my way with my feet because God only knew what might be at the bottom. I started shivering, but it did not matter. Once the fighting started, I would warm up soon enough. I was surprised when the water only came up to my chin, and the next step was a little shallower. The edge, when I reached it, was slick and muddy. I wriggled out on my stomach and lay flat on the ground, so cold that I gritted my teeth to keep them from chattering.

James tapped my shoulder to let me know he was out of the water. I tapped his in response and pushed myself to my hands and knees. Crawling would make the wooden steps and the grappling hook clatter on the ground, so I slowly rose to my feet. A silent prayer to Saint Bride, and I was ready. I felt for the castle wall and pressed my back against it. It took a minute to straighten the rope of the ladder. There were shuffling sounds from the darkness. It took two men to raise the ladder, each with a spear point through a hole in one of the hooks.

James felt along the hook. "Got it," he whispered.

A chirrup of a frog. A moment later, another from farther down. I bumped James' shoulder as a signal. It was a wonder the guards, who had to be up there somewhere, could not hear my heart thudding or the fast rasp of my breath. I gripped the spear and eased it upward until my arms were stretched over my head. The damned hook had to catch on the edge of the parapet. James hissed, sucking air through his teeth as we jiggled the spears. I felt them catch. Tugged hard to be sure. There was no way to know in the dark if the others had.

Someone up above shouted, "What was that?"

My heart was trying to beat its way out of my chest as I scrambled up the ladder one-handed, the spear in my left hand. I stuck the butt through the crenel and used it as a lever to jump through. James brushed my back as he followed. My men jumped and sprawled through the crenels onto the parapet walk.

A mail-clad man-at-arms with a torch in his shield hand stood a few strides away. He froze for a moment, then shouted, "'Ware the—"

My spear went through his throat. He was gurgling as I dragged his sword the rest of the way out of his scabbard and took a moment to slide my arm into the strap of his shield.

A tower door opened and faint light silhouetted of men rushing out.

I raised my looted shield. The first guard in chainmail but no aventail reached me. I slashed his throat. Then another guardsman swung his sword. I caught the blade on my own. Blood dripped down the guard's chest, a sword all the way through from the back. "Got him!" Ashkirk yelled. He kicked the man to jerk his sword from his hand and picked it up. The dying guard groaned, and I struck to finish him. James kicked another body off the parapet walk, slick with rain mixed with blood.

Another enemy, a knight in plate armor, bellowing with wordless fury, rushed me, driving down an overhead blow that would have split my chest to groin. I jumped to the side, pommeled my sword, and hammered the hilt onto the top of his head. His head stove in like a broken eggshell, and he went down. I switched my grip to the hilt and slammed a blow to the back of his mail-clad knee. The man screamed as he fell face-first off the walk.

"Attackers!" The shout came from the bailey. "Attackers on the rampart!" A bell started tolling the alarm.

There was a flash of metal. I flinched as a crossbow bolt whacked into a merlon beside me. One of my men screamed. A crossbowman frantically cranked the handle of his weapon. I ran at him, pommeled my blade, and knocked it from his hands with a down strike. He swayed back to pull his blade free. I hacked from left to right, slitting his throat to the backbone. He collapsed in a spray of blood.

I bellowed, "For the King!" and ran toward the stairs down to the bailey.

Men in armor, weapons in hand, were flooding out the door and down the steps from the donjon. Some raced for the stables.

My men swarmed onto the walk. A spear clattered on the ground, and James grabbed it as he ran. I sprinted, taking the steps to the bailey two at a time. I speared the first snarling face through the eye with the point of my sword. The man screamed and fell away. Gil was to my left, scything his sword as though reaping grain. James jumped down to the bailey and knocked a defender down when he landed on top of him.

"Open the gate!" I bellowed, and I spiked a man about to attack him. My blade stuck and tore from my hands when the man fell. Gil lunged and hacked another man down to give me time to jerk the sword free.

Torches flickered next to the door to the donjon, and light flashed on sword blade and spear point. Colbyn drove his spear through a defender's belly. One tried to kill me with his ax, mouth wide as he shouted curses. Gil killed the man, thrusting his spear into the gaping mouth so that the curses ended with a gush of blood.

Then amid the defenders stood my cousin, the Earl of

Douglas, fully armed and armored for combat. Only his eyes, gleaming with rage, showed through the slit in his helm. He snarled and came at me. I swayed back and then stepped in. Our swords met, the hilts binding. He pushed downward. I eased his pressure and cut for his wrist, where the armor was weak.

He knew his business. He turned into my cut and caught the sword on his hilt. Wary of a pommel strike, I disengaged. He pressed his attack, swinging again and again. I caught the blade on my hilt and flipped his hands to swing at his neck. His sword grated on his gorget and knocked him sideways. He backed up a step.

Behind me, horses' hooves pounded across the wooden bridge like a thousand drums. "A Bruce! A Bruce!" David shouted. Around me was chaos. The Douglas's men fought back with wild savagery.

I went at my cousin. He swung with all his weight from the side. Our swords slammed together. I grappled him and slammed the flat of my sword side into his chest, pushing him back. But a crowd of men-at-arms came to their lord's defense, screaming, "A Douglas! A Douglas!"

A blow hit me on the back of the head. I flew forward as Douglas's sword swished past me. My head bounced on the ground, the wind knocked out of me. Gasping for air and expecting a killing blow, I rolled. But the Douglas was swinging onto a mount, surrounded by a score of his men on horses. One hoof barely missed my sword hand. I rolled sideways to get out of the way as they spurred toward the bridge.

More trying to fight their way to the stables faced us, screaming in defiance. I rolled out of the way of a sword strike and speared upward, beneath his mail hauberk, into his belly. Ashkirk was with him, screaming, "For Scotland!" as he slashed into the crowd. Colbyn fought to his left.

Shamefully, I used my sword like a cane to stagger to my

feet. Another man thrust a spear at me. I knocked the spear downward and backslashed at the face framed by a battered steel helm. He twisted aside. I stepped over a body and thrust as hard as I could into his left eye. A knight, bellowing curses, charged me. James smashed his head in with an ax. Blood gushed into my face, and I shook my head to get it out of my eyes.

Alexander Scrymgeour, his horse snorting and pawing, waved the royal banner over his head. Our men shouted and cheered as they killed. The rest of the Douglas' men, staring death in the face, broke. Some ran for the parapet and leaped from the curtain wall, but the rest shouted that they surrendered. They threw down their swords and spears and knelt to beg for mercy.

The marischal yelled for the prisoners to be stripped and bound, and guards posted on the ramparts.

I strode to the nearest kneeling man and grabbed him by the throat. "Where is Lord Haliburton?" I screamed and shook him like a rag doll.

"Down. Cells are in the undercroft."

I shoved him, and he landed on his back. I turned my back and headed toward the door of the keep. The stairs to the undercroft would be within.

One of the prisoners, face bloodied, yelled, "Lord King, I can give you news that will be of value to you. I beg you to show me mercy."

David turned and snarled, "Do you try to bargain with me, worm?"

"No! No, no, sire. I only ask you to remember that I aided you. I was in the keep when a messenger brought news to Lord Douglas."

"What news?"

"Robert Ramsay and his men were ambushed near Inverkeithing. He was taken prisoner."

That was serious news, if true. Scrubbing my face with my hand, I tried to make sense of it. "Who took him prisoner? Who was leading them?" It could not have been my cousin unless he had found some magical means of travel.

"I dinnae ken, my lord."

Tipping my head back and closing my eyes, I took a long breath. Fatigue rolled over me like a wave of the sea. I turned to Colbyn. "Braw work. Tell the men I said so and that they will be rewarded. And let them rest. Tell Domhnall to take out his scouts and track Douglas. I want to ken which way he is going."

The marischal barked to one of his serjeants, "Haul these men to the dungeons and release Sir Walter and any of his men locked up." He turned and followed the King into the keep.

Inside, David stood next to the table on the dais, a parchment in his hand with three seals dangling from it. The other tables had been taken apart to give men room to room to rest. He threw the parchment down. "Poisonous knaves!"

"What is it?" The marischal asked.

"Treason!" He jabbed his finger at the document. "It is an indenture planning my overthrow."

I strode to the dais and sniffed a flagon of wine. It had a hint of cherries and lilac. I filled a pewter goblet and handed it to the king. He took it with a hand that was shaking and drank deeply. I then filled goblets for the marischal and me.

"Between?" I asked. I could guess, but I wanted to know for sure.

"Who else?" The King ground his teeth. "Douglas, Dunbar, and my beloved heir. Robert Stewart."

"They must have thought they could move before we learned what they were up to." The marischal swirled the wine in his goblet. "And it might have worked if one of

Walter's men-at-arms had not reached us. We owe that man a reward."

Sir Walter limped in, his face mottled with bruises. "Your Grace! Thanks be to God, you are all right!" He took the king's hand and bowed over it. "I am shamed that they took me unawares."

"You couldnae have expected such treachery." David drained his wine goblet and slammed it down. "I expected them to face me like men, not stab me in the back like the veriest scullions."

I took a deep drink. It warmed my belly and spread through my aching body like a caress. "Now we must decide what to do. I sent my scouts to find out which way Douglas fled." I scratched my beard. "Hermitage Castle or mayhap Hawick are the most likely. He will want to run where he can gather more men. But that news about Robert Ramsay. It means there is another army to the north. Probably Strathearn's."

"Aye," the lord marischal growled. "And if we chase Douglas, we invite an attack on our rear."

"But if we dinnae, we give him a chance to gather more of his men."

Sir Walter poured wine and drank as more men filed into the hall. "I suggest we let our men eat and rest, bandage our wounds, and wait for news from your scouts." He grimaced. "I could use a meal and a good night's sleep as well."

"Or...I could take my men and find Robert Stewart." I smiled, the idea warming me even more than the wine. "And you give chase to the Douglas."

The marischal said, "I dinnae like the idea of splitting our forces."

"By then, Erskine and Campbell should have caught up with you. With those and Sir Walter's men, my splitting off willnae leave you lacking men."

"You only have a hundred and fifty men,"

It was a true observation, but I smiled. "I havenae intention of challenging them to battle. I must see where he is and the lie of the land. Then I will decide on either an ambush or a rear attack." I shrugged. "It is the fighting I am best at."

CHAPTER TWENTY-FIVE

The Next Day Near Queensferry, Scotland

I lay in the damp heather, and a gray ghost hawk glided overhead with the blood of its last meal on its belly and talons. The rain had ceased about dawn, and now only a few clouds scudded across the sky. My men relaxed, many dozing, in the small clearing. After a day's ride to Dirleton Castle, a night battle, and a hard day's ride almost to Queensferry, they deserved it. And I wanted both men and horses fit for yet another fight. We had come out of the fight at the castle better than I had expected. Only two men killed and some minor injuries. Now I awaited Domhnall's return with his small group of fellow scouts.

"My lord."

I sat up. Domhnall could move with remarkable silence.

The man who dropped to a knee was a year or two older than me, his skin weathered like any outdoorsman, and his hair dark. His thick brows were drawn together. "I found them with nae trouble. Barnbougle didnae put up much of a fight. After it surrendered, they settled in for the night. By the horns and noise, they be about to march." His mouth crooked in a sly smile. "Happens a messenger was seeking them yestereve."

I raised my eyebrows.

"Found me instead." He pulled a piece of parchment from the scrip that hung from his belt.

It was short, to the point, and had my cousin's seal at the bottom.

"Good man." I rose to my feet. "What banners? And how many men?"

"The Stewart's checky banner. His and his sons' banners. A few lesser pennants I couldnae put a name to. I would say three hundred men." He wobbled his head back and forth. "Mayhap three hundred fifty."

"So Robert Stewart willnae ken the Douglas has lost Dirleton." I tapped my chin. "I expect they will make for the old Roman Road to find Douglas." There was no way to know if they planned to meet at Dirleton, but Stewart would be bound to move in that direction. "I will follow at a distance. Watch for a good place for an attack where they cannae flank us." Keeping me apprised was his job, so I had no need to tell him to bring me reports. Domhnall touched his fingers to his forehead, knowing exactly what I was looking for.

Only seven knights were with me. Gil was good enough with a lance. He could act as one of the wedge and I would be the point. The men-at-arms would use sword or axe as we cut through our enemies. I would hold the archers back, and they could take down any who tried to flee—except for Robert Stewart and his sons. Those I wanted alive.

When one of the scouts brought word that Stewart's force had passed us, we handed out lances and followed, the Pentland Hills rising before us. The rain had left the road muddy, so there was no worry that dust would reveal our presence. I held us at an amble, our helms off for comfort, not wanting to tire our mounts or overtake our enemy with the scouts ahead and to both flanks. Twice we briefly stopped to water and rest our horses before we went on.

The sun had just started its downward path when Domhnall raced back to us, horse's mane flying. "They are almost between the hills ahead. The sides are too steep and craggy for the horses to climb."

"You took out their scouts?"

He grinned.

"Perfect."

I put on my helm and fastened it, which was clumsy with my gauntlets on. It would quickly turn into an oven under the heat of the sun, but that could not be helped. My heart was hammering as it always did before a fight.

We formed a wedge with me at the point. James and Gil rode at my horse's withers. For a wedge to work, you must ride with your horses, almost touching as you go from a walk to a canter to a gallop. Properly done, the weight of the formation could smash anything in front of it or cut through an army. Perfectly done, you could turn and smash through again.

"Steady now," I yelled. "Stay together, and no one breaks into a canter until I shout charge. The weight of the wedge has to cut through them, and we kill as we go. Once we are on the other side, we turn. If you get out of position, try to catch up."

We went forward at a walk, and I looped my reins around my pommel. When the rear of the Stewart's column came into sight, I called, "Couch lances." and urged my horse to a canter. My gray was strained to be let loose. It only took a squeeze of my calves, and it plunged to a gallop.

As we closed, I bellowed, "For Scotland and King David!"

They were desperately hauling on reins and trying to turn. We hit them with a crash of lances and snorting, rearing horses. Their mounts were bowled over and men thrown.

There were screams as they were trampled by our mounts or their own. My lance hit a knight in the middle of the back and sent him over his horse's head. The next managed to turn and took the blow on his shield, rocked sideways in the saddle, but I was already past, carried by my momentum. Another caught my lance on his shield, and it shattered, so I dragged my claymore free, aiming it like a lance.

The air was full of screams and crashes of lance and sword. Dirt and scree flew in the air from pounding hooves. Gil stayed on my right and protected me from sword thrusts as I raised my own sword to strike. A blue and white checky shield was in front of me. I slammed my sword over the shield's rim. It rocked him back but slid over the smooth metal. I spurred ahead.

There was a clear space in front of me. I spurred ahead and risked a look over my shoulder. Most of our men were locked in fighting with only a score still in the wedge. I gave a mental shrug. It took practice to stay together through such a charge. I leaned to the left and used my legs to make a wide turn, losing only a little speed, and charged back the way we had come.

I pointed with my sword at the yellow and blue checky banner in the middle of the fray. "Yon! We must take that!"

The first man in front of me, unhorsed, froze. He did not even try to run before I ran him down. The screams of horses and men were deafening. To my front, several Stewart knights closed ranks around the Stewart. "Protect your lord!" someone bellowed.

With my claymore level, my hit lifted the next man out of the saddle, hurling him backward. He hurtled, flailing, into two men behind him. Their horses jibbed and reared. James shouldered his horse into a man-at-arms who thrust a spear at me. Seeing my chance, I spurred my gray into the gap. I turned a blow with my shield as I hacked the pole holding the banner aloft. It fell, and I trampled it under my horse's hooves.

Head bare and sword in his hand, Robert Stewart was right before me. I saluted the earl and urged the sweat-covered gray forward.

The thin-faced heir to the throne of Scotland threw down his sword. "I yield!" he shouted. "I yield! Lay down your weapons!"

Some of his men obeyed, casting their swords and spears aside. Even more broke and ran.

I bowed to the earl and said, "My lord, it will be my honor to escort you and your sons to Edinburgh, where comfortable chambers await you." I made sure I did not smirk since making even more of an enemy of the man who might still eventually be King did not seem wise.

CHAPTER TWENTY-SIX

Two Days Later outside Hermitage Castle

There were chambers suitable for prisoners, as comfortable as any in the keep. However, they had arrow slits for windows and good bolts on the outside of thick, iron-bound doors. Colbyn chose men to guard them, two to a shift. They would stay where I put them until the King said otherwise. A single night's rest for horses and men saw us off to find King David at Hermitage Castle, where a messenger said he would be.

The castle where I had grown up had changed enormously over the years. The years the English held it had seen it strengthened and enlarged, so now it was a substantial gray stone fortress. Around it stretched an army lazing in the mild spring air but holding those within like a steel trap. I told Colbyn to have the men rest and eat but delay making camp until I had orders.

The Douglas banner hung listlessly over the keep, so we knew where my cousin was, sulking inside. But where was the Earl of Dunbar?

David laughed when I told him I had locked up Stewart and his sons in Edinburgh.

I tilted my head toward the castle. "How long do you think this will take?"

"You ken the place better than I. You tell me."

I squinted at the solid walls. "It has a good well, so they willnae run out of water. The question is how much food they have and how many mouths to feed." I barked a laugh. "And how impatient my cousin is. He isnae a good one for sitting still and waiting."

David tugged on his short, pointed beard. "I willnae speak to him, but I want you to." His eyes gleamed with amusement. "Apologize for having struck him as he is the head of your family. And mention that his friend, the Earl of Strathearn, is a guest at Edinburgh Castle."

I coughed. "Och, he should take that well."

At the king's smirk, I sent a herald to ask for a conference on the bridge.

Douglas's plate gleamed in the sunlight without a scratch. If it had taken any harm when we fought, I could not see it. His scowl, however, was as black as our family's name.

His face was weathered, and deep lines ran from his nose to his chin. He was not a man given too much smiling, but at forty, he was as much a brawny knight beneath that steel as he had ever been. My horse's hooves thudded on the wooden drawbridge. I had thought to wear armor to speak to him, but instead, I changed into a slightly wrinkled tunic and hose, and Gil dug out a chaperon with a tail that draped to my shoulder. You did not wear armor to discuss peace.

I drew up and bowed. With total insincerity but a straight face, I said, "My lord. I must give you my apology. I shouldnae have struck you at Dirleton. For that, I beg your forgiveness." The things I did for my king.

He raised his heavy, black eyebrows. "And that is why you asked for a meeting?"

"It merely needed to be said." Because I was commanded to say it, but I did not mention that. My cousin had never understood me and never would, I was sure. "The King wished you to be told that the Earl of Strathearn is well and a guest at Edinburgh Castle, along with his sons. He feared you might be concerned for the earl's safety. He assures you that when you yield, he will also pledge your safety as well."

His smile did not reach his eyes. "To think that I offered to allow you to be part of our party and to aid us. I should have kent better than to trust a bastard."

"Aye, Liddesdale made that mistake." The memory scalded like acid. "He made the mistake of trusting both of us."

A look of rage flashed across his face. "Like you, he was a traitor. He deserved the death I gave him."

My hands were shaking with anger at least as great as his. I took a deep breath. This was no time for it. "William," I rarely called him by name, so it gave him pause. "The rebellion is over. You cannae win without the Stewart. How many mouths to feed do you have inside that castle? How long can your food last? You cannae survive on well water. Yield, and the King will allow you to renew your fealty. It may humiliate you, but you and your men will be alive. He doesnae intend to forfeit your lands."

"But you must watch your back for when Dunbar raises my men from my score of castles."

He wheeled his black charger and cantered back through the gate. The chains of the portcullis grated as it fell. I glanced up at the bows poking between the merlons, but I did not even flinch from the glares on my back as I rode back to the king.

Turning my horse's head back to the siege line, I could

feel the eyes on my back from the ramparts. But if he allowed them to kill me, someone might say he did it from fear. That he would never allow.

Back at the camp, I tossed my reins to Gil. The lord marischal looked on as I turned to David. "He says he expects relief from Dunbar," I said.

Reginald Keith, lord marischal of Scotland, snorted. "You jest."

I gnawed my lip, thinking because I was sure he did not believe what he had said. Suddenly I realized what probably should have been obvious. "He is too proud to yield before Dunbar does. He was humiliated at Dirleton. If he waits, at least he will have been the last to yield."

The marischal spat on the ground. "Dunbar willnae try to rescue Douglas, but he may need assurance you willnae forfeit his titles and lands. Those mean more to the bull's-pizzle than any alliance."

"Do we even ken where Dunbar is? Has he attacked anything? Any word at all?" I asked.

"If he has gone to ground in Dunbar Castle, it would take a year to starve him out." David threw up his hands. "And I dinnae even want to. Now that their conspiracy is destroyed and my power proven, they arenae danger to me." He gave me a significant look. "And I have a task for you that this is delaying."

"It is a pity Lady Agnes has died." I had been very fond of that strong-minded lady who had acted as her husband's backbone, which he lacked. I pinched the bridge of my nose and sighed. "I was a guest there in the past. I feel sure he will offer me guest rights. He kens I wouldnae violate them, and I can assure him of your promise. He is highly unlikely to try to kill me. Unlike my cousin."

"Are you sure, Archie?" The marischal asked. "We could

send a herald to carry word. It is beneath you to act as a messenger."

"He might believe a messenger. But he might not. Lady Agnes liked me and that carries weight with him. He will believe me if I give him my oath." Like many who had broken their own word, he did not trust easily. "But let Douglas stew. I need a night's rest before I ride halfway across Scotland."

A week later, it was almost comedic when Dunbar grudgingly accompanied me back to Hermitage Castle. Wizened and wrinkled as he was, he was still a wiry old knight. He pulled his sleek mount up before the castle and shouted, "You knotty-pated fool! We have lost, so come out and yield."

CHAPTER TWENTY-SEVEN

Two Weeks Later, Edinburgh Castle

The vast great hall of Edinburgh Castle was full of a noisy and glittering crowd. At the head of the room on a raised dais sat King David on his throne with Bishop Bur, Bishop de Landallis, the recently forgiven Earl of Mar, the abbot of Melrose, the lord marischal, and Erskine, the chancellor, and Sir Robert Ramsay.

Joanna's smile was a little tremulous, and she put her hand to her chest. "I hope nae ever to have such a few days again. What a relief when you returned."

"Aye," I said, "it isnae something I would care to repeat." I nudged James. "But James saw that nae harm came to me."

He snorted, and I suspected he was remembering the Douglas nearly trampling me in the bailey of Dirleton Castle. No battle was certain in its outcome until it was over, nor was any knight so skilled that he might not die.

She gave him a soft smile. "Then Sir James, I thank you."

James gave a deep bow. "My sincerest pleasure, my lady." He grinned. "Even if his lordship exaggerates."

A little page scurried through the crowd and bobbed a

bow to me. "My lord, please, His Grace requires you to join him."

I nodded to my wife and followed the lad to the dais. I made my obeisance to the King, who nodded to the herald.

Three trumpets blared a noisy flourish, and a herald shouted, "Sir Robert Stewart, Earl of Strathearn, William Douglas, Earl of Douglas, and Patrick Cospatrick, Earl of Dunbar, are called before the most gracious lord, David, King of Scots."

The main door of the hall was thrown open. The three walked in. Like the parting of the Red Sea, an opening formed for them. A buzz of speculation ran around the room.

The Earl of Douglas climbed the steps and stiffly dropped to his knees. Bishop de Landallis handed him a parchment to read.

David looked on impassively as Douglas took a new oath.

"I shall assist and defend all proceedings begun by my Lord King and his ministers or whomsoever he calls his loyal men with all my strength against all men who live, move, or die."

He looked up, and his face flushed scarlet. In a choked voice, he continued. "This is notwithstanding whatever oaths I may have made with Patrick, Earl of Dunbar, or Robert, Earl of Strathearn. I give my oath that I will not work with them or any other without first letting my Lord King know and requesting his license under pain of losing my lands and lordships and of facing perjury, dishonor, cancellation of my knighthood, and defacement of my arms."

He made a stiff obeisance and walked to the side. Patrick of Dunbar gave the same oath. There were a few gasps when Robert Stewart's oath contained a provision that if he broke his oath, he would be stricken from the succession to the kingdom of Scotland.

But at last, it was over, and squires and pages in the royal livery scurried in carrying flagons and goblets of wine. Tables were set up along the walls that soon groaned with food that filled the air with the scents of roasted meat and spices. Joanna strolled through the crowd to join us and I tucked her hand in my elbow.

David took a goblet of claret from one of the pages and said, "Archie, I told you that I have a new task for you."

"You did, sire. As always, I am at your service." My mouth was suddenly dry, and I bit down on a smile. Whatever it was, it would not be easy, but it would be worth the cost.

"You have often told me that the Galloway rebellion must be ended. I agree with you. I relieve you of Edinburgh Castle, and I am sending you to end their defiance."

I opened my mouth and then closed it.

"When you succeed, I will give Galloway to you." His eyes crinkled with his broad smile, eyes shining. "Lord of Galloway will be your new title."

Joanna gasped. Lord of Galloway was one of the most major titles in Scotland.

"I willnae fail you, Your Grace. I give you my oath on it." My heart was pounding so hard the great hall should echo with the sound.

A Few Weeks Later

The two wains, one of mattress and clothes, the other Wilikyn and his nursemaid, no longer a wet nurse, cushioned with an extra mattress and linens, made the trip to Drumsagard Castle in Lanark take longer than it might have. Fortunately, Joanna was cheerful company along with James on the way. Eventually, the lad ran out of birds to name and hares to point at. He grew cranky from being confined, but his nurse knew countless rhyming games.

Tapping his face, she chanted, "Brow, brow, brinkie, nose, nose, nebbie. Chin, chin, chuckle, Curry-wurry! Curry-wurry!" and tickled his belly, sending him into raptures of giggles until he fell over. That made me guffawed, which made Joanna chuckle.

Two of the Flemings, recently knighted, had joined my following and looked on with baffled amusement. James and Ashkirk just grinned. I had decided, against all custom, that Gil should be knighted, but it would be best done after a battle. A hundred men-at-arms led by Colbyn followed.

I gazed into the sun-drenched distance. "Drumsagard will do for now, but I have plans. I dinnae ken how long rebuilding Bothwell Castle will take. But as soon as I can find a good mason, I will have him start on it." Bothwell had once been one of the greatest castles in Scotland. It would be again.

Her mouth twitched. "While you are off becoming the lion of Galloway?"

"Mayhap only to conquer it."

Thanks for reading! If you enjoyed this novel, please consider a taking a minute or two of your valuable time to leave an honest review at your favorite retailer.

HISTORICAL NOTES

The exact date that Archibald Douglas became Guardian of Edinburgh Castle and Sheriff of Lothian is debatable. I have found it given anywhere between 1358 and 1362. In 1362, he definitely was given the responsibility of bringing Galloway under King David's control, so it seems a safe assumption that it cannot be as late as 1362. For the sake of narrative, I used the earliest possible date. Another minor change is the name of the Marischal of Scotland, who was yet another William, William Keith. I long since lost count of the noblemen of the period named William. To put it mildly, this is inconvenient for a historical fiction writer.

Another event that has no definitive date is the birth of Archibald's illegitimate son, William of Nithsdale. Working back from the date at which he is first referred to as a knight taking part in combat, it is likely that he was born around 1360 and that fit in well with the novel's timeline. As is typical of the period, there is no record of his mother, allowing me to use my imagination.

Most of the other events in the novel are well established. The one that makes me shake my head is his challenge to fight for the hand of Joanna of Moravia. This is a recorded fact, not something I made up, as unlikely as it seems. I suspect it was more political than romantic or 'chivalrous'. That as her husband Archibald had rightful claim to the vast lands she inherited from both her father and her late husband, I am convinced, was behind this remarkable episode. He, in effect, forced anyone who objected to face him on the field.

The second wave of the Great Plague that hit Scotland in 1361 may have been even worse than the first wave. There was certainly a higher mortality rate amongst the nobility and estimates are that about a third of the population of Scotland died that year.

King David's suppression of the earls' rebellion was fast and complete. Despite this, his response was a temperate one, so temperate that it was remarked on and praised by chroniclers at some length. He was praised for his mildness and mercy. However, executing or seizing the lands of Scotland's most powerful nobles would have simply incited more rebellion. It was no doubt a wise decision, putting him in a powerful position, but of course, the thorny problem of the dispute over an heir was not solved.

King David's most controversial acts were his repeated negotiations to name an English prince as an heir, failing an heir of his body to replace Robert Stewart. The deep-seated hatred between the two men can hardly be overstated. Some claim that the negotiations show that King David had become 'pro-English' or too friendly with England's King Edward. I consider this an absurd argument. While he may or may not have liked King Edward III, there is absolutely no reason to doubt that he wanted to have a child of his own to inherit his throne. He was still a relatively young man at the time of this novel and expected to have children.

There is no record of what David thought of King

Edward. They shared a strong interest in jousting and chivalric pursuits, so they may have had good feelings. They were both devotees of Thomas a Beckett, as well. However, Edward's confinement of him was stringent at several lengthy periods when David was allowed absolutely no contact with his own subjects, which could hardly have increased good feelings.

A much more likely explanation for the proposal was that it was simply a way of putting off payment of a ransom that was crippling financially for Scotland. As long as there were ongoing negotiations on Edward's son inheriting the throne of Scotland, it gave David a much-improved negotiating position. Did David consider there to be any chance at all that the Scottish Parliament, which had threatened to dethrone David rather than agree, would change its mind? Personally, I find that unlikely. Whatever King David's flaws, there is no indication that he was stupid.

The genuine mystery of King David's reign was his love affair with Katherine Mortimer. She was often referred to as being English, which I find unlikely. It has come to be disputed for the same reasons that I find it dubious. There is no record of her as a member of a noble family or part of the royal court. David did not wander the streets of England, so that he would meet random English commoners. He was very much a prisoner with limited contacts. I believe that the early references to her as English were a fairly natural but mistaken assumption that because she returned with him from England that she was English. While there were Mortimers in England, there was also a family of Mortimers in Scotland who held lands and a barony. David would have been more likely to meet and have the chance to fall in love with one of his wife's ladies-in-waiting. I find that a plausible explanation.

That does not explain her murder. There is no record of her influencing David's decisions or of large gifts to her or her family, so the motive for a conspiracy to murder her is baffling. One explanation is simply that she was pregnant. Her child might have cut the Stewarts out of the line of succession and raised her family to unwanted prominence. That, of course, would have required the child to be legitimatized, which was something that could be done once Queen Joan was divorced or had died.

If you would be interested in reading some source material about the period and about Archibald Douglas, Walter Bower's *Scoticronicon* is essential for this period. Aberdeen University Press published an excellent complete series with the Latin and an English translation, but finding the set is difficult. I am fortunate to own it. The extensive detail in Michael Penman's *David II* can be tedious. I also disagree with some of his claims and conclusions, but it is worth reading for the depth of his research. For a full understanding of the role of the Douglases, I recommend *The Black Douglases* by Michael Brown. Another essential reference for the period is John Froissart's *Chronicles of England, France, Spain, and the Adjoining Countries,* an intimidatingly massive work. Since Froissart was acquainted with Archibald Douglas, having been his guest while traveling in Scotland, the descriptions of Archie in the chronicle are particularly interesting. And, of course, I always have reference to the *Scots Peerage*. Once again, I recommend *Fabulous Feasts* by Madeleine Pelner Cosman for anyone interested in medieval food and meals.

GLOSSARY

- Afeart—(Scots) Afraid.
- Anent—Regarding, about.
- Anyroad—(Scots) Anyway.
- Ave—Hail, an expression of greeting, although Latin was commonly used in the Middle Ages.
- Aventail—Detachable mail hung from a helmet to protect the neck and shoulders.
- Aye—Yes.
- Bailey yard—The defended area around a castle keep.
- Bairn—(Scots) Baby.
- Bannock—(Scots) An unleavened flatbread made with oats usually cooked on a griddle.
- Bascinet—Helm that was fully visored, often conical, but often worn without the visor for improved visibility and ventilation. Worn with an aventail.
- Bide—Remain or stay somewhere.
- Brae—(Scots)A hillside or sloping bank.
- Braw—(Scots) Fine.

- Burgh—(Scots) An autonomous chartered town. Burghs had rights to representation in the Parliament of Scotland.
- Burgher—A citizen of a town or city, typically a merchant of substance.
- Cannae—(Scots) Cannot.
- Canny—(Scots) Careful, prudent.
- Checky—In heraldry, a fess divided into squares of two tinctures, like a checkerboard.
- Cervelliere—Steel skull cap worn as a helm.
- Cotehardie—A long-sleeved, close-fitting, belted medieval outer garment that was usually thigh-length for men and full-length for women.
- Cuirass—Covers the chest, not the back, but the name is sometimes used to describe the chest and back plates together.
- Depute—(Scots) Deputy.
- Dinnae—(Scots) Do not.
- Ecu—An Old French unit of value.
- Enarmes—The strap by which a shield was held on the forearm.
- Fess—In heraldry, a band on a coat of arms or banner running horizontally across the center of the shield.
- Forbye—Besides, in addition.
- Good brother—Brother-in-law.
- Good weal—The public good, the good of society.
- Guige— A long strap, typically made of leather, used to hang a shield on the shoulder or neck when not in use. In combat, it allowed the use of a two-handed weapon without discarding the shield.
- Harling—A rough wall finish of lime and aggregate. Many castles in Scotland have walls finished with harling.

- Hauberk—Mail shirt reaching to the mid-thigh with sleeves.
- Haubergeon—Generally refers to the quilted garment worn under a hauberk, but the terms are sometimes used interchangeably.
- Hell mend (someone)—A curse expressing anger, usually that someone will not heed a warning.
- Herschip—(Scots) Plundering, devastation especially the carrying off of cattle but usually includes more extensive burning and devastation.
- Hie—Go quickly; hasten.
- Houppelande—An outer garment, with a long, full body and flaring sleeves, worn by both men and women in Europe in the late Middle Ages, often lined with fur.
- Ken—(Scots) Know.
- Kent—(Scots) Knew; past tense of 'ken'.
- Kist—(Scots) A strong box, typically made of wood used for storage or shipping, a chest.
- Love-bairn—(Scots) A child born out of wedlock.
- Mosstrooper—Another word for a reiver, a raider along the Anglo-Scottish border.
- Och— (Scots) An exclamation of surprise, confirmation, or disagreement depending on context.
- Recet— (Anglo-Norman French) Literally means "Place of receiving" and was the term used for the tent where jousters retired to rest or to prepare for a bout.
- Reiver—A raider along the Anglo-Scottish border.
- Rerebrace—Plate armor that covered the lower arm.
- Rig—Arable strip of land separated by uncultivated strips of grassland.

- Sabaton—Foot coverings generally in mail or plate.
- Sassenach—(Scots) Derogatory term for an Englishman.
- Scrip—A small bag or wallet.
- Sheriff—The king's highest representative in a county, responsible for collecting local taxes and for maintaining law and order.
- Siller—(Scots) Silver, usually refers to coins or money.
- Skelp—(Scots) A blow, slap, smack.
- Smirr—(Scots) A very fine, drifting rain.
- Tolbooth—(Scots) The main municipal building of a medieval Scots burgh
- Undercroft—A vault or chamber under the ground.
- Wattle-- Material for making fences, walls, etc., consisting of stakes woven with twigs or branches.
- Willnae—(Scots) Will not
- Withy—A tough, flexible willow branch, used for tying, binding, and basketry.
- Yon—(Scots) That or those (objects or people)

www.ingramcontent.com/pod-product-compliance
Lightning Source LLC
Chambersburg PA
CBHW070206160726
47997CB00017B/442